Nick

JUSTICE SERIES BOOK 2

KATHI S. BARTON

World Castle Publishing, LLC
Pensacola, Florida

Copyright © Kathi S. Barton 2015
Hardback ISBN: 9781629892979
Print ISBN: 9781629892986
eBook ISBN: 9781629892993
First Edition World Castle Publishing, LLC, July 10, 2015
http://www.worldcastlepublishing.com

Licensing Notes

Cover: Karen Fuller
Editor: Eric Johnston
Editor: Maxine Bringenberg

CHAPTER 1

"I swear to you if you say that to me one more time, not only am I going to break your face, but I might just put you someplace deep and dark and forget about you." Joel Delaney stretched his neck and felt it pop several times before he looked at the man in front of him. "Now. We're going to try this again. Where the fuck is Addison West? And if you say one word about her being lost to me, I swear to Christ, I will kill you."

"Last time anybody ever saw her was when she went to the dress shop and then the bank. There she cleaned out her account. And that was five years ago, or thereabouts. There wasn't much in there, but she was in there for a while. I had me a look and so far as I can tell, she made one phone call to her grandmother. Then she just seemed to be gone. Nobody's heard from her since. If she did any more, nobody is saying." Joel knew about her account. Her parents had set her up a checking account when Addison turned sixteen. It had been their way of saying to the world that they trusted their daughter with money. But so far as her father and he knew, there had never been any more than about a grand in the account at any given time. "I tried to get in to see Mrs. Simon-English, but she's not having it. Stubborn old broad if you ask me."

Joel knew the stubborn old broad too. Evangeline Simon-English was the most annoying, pain in the ass woman he'd ever had the displeasure of meeting. But he treated her like the queen that she thought she was to try to keep on her good side. She was frighteningly rich, and he wanted her to at least respect him enough to have a party in his name. He supposed with as much money as she had, she could be whatever she wanted. Evie to her close friends, she was the grande dame of all the world. But he'd had to call her Mrs. Simon-English since he met her, and made the mistake of calling her Evie when it was announced that he was going to marry Addison. That hadn't gone over any better than him trying to kiss her hand. She'd slapped him right on the face for touching her.

"You will have respect for me, Joel Delaney. I'm not one of those women that you are frequently chasing around your desk." He started to deny it, but she held up her hand and told him not to even try. "I know a great deal about you and your family. And I don't like you one bit. If my granddaughter loves you, which I doubt, then I will have to tolerate you. But she doesn't, so that will be the extent of our relationship. None whatsoever. You are not welcome in my homes, nor—and I daresay it will never come to this— will you be welcome into my family."

"She doesn't have to love me, Mrs. Simon-English, but she will obey me." The old bitch, the fucking bat as he called her when referring to her, just huffed at him. "My influence and money will be enough to keep her in the style that she's grown up with, but I will not tolerate you interfering in our lives once the wedding has taken place.

And she won't be coming to you for anything. I'll cut that off as well."

"You can dream a big dream, can't you?" She moved away from him, but not before turning to stare at him. "You'd do well to remember who I am, Mr. Delaney. While you may have some money, I have a great deal more. And I'm not afraid to use it to get anything and everything I want."

That had been nearly five years ago. The next day his fiancée was gone and no one had seen her since. Her parents, about as useless as some of the shits that worked for him, had no idea where their daughter had gone. And as far as he could see, they didn't care either. Once she'd left, they'd cut her off without a dime and had written her out of their lives as if she'd never been there. But he had a feeling that the fucking old bat not only knew where she was, but was funding her as well. No way could Addison be without money. She was a rich woman and would want money all the time.

Joel knew next to nothing about Addison. Not that he cared, other than for what she brought to his home in the form of money. Other than he wanted her as his wife, and her money. He knew that she'd been twenty-one when she'd left him, and that she was beautiful beyond measure.

Not that he really needed her money, but the point was there was never enough of it. He had made good investments, owned a business that made money, and he had a lovely house that she'd be taking care of. He had plenty of money of his own, yes that was true. But having more, like her parents did, was something that he wanted and would have. And having the prestige of having the name West attached to his was going to open doors like he'd never realized before.

When Burt left him a few minutes later, Joel made his way to his play room. He'd been summoned away from his fun and when he returned, he was going to go on as if nothing had happened. The woman he had tied to his bed was lying just as he'd left her.

Her legs were spread wide and her breasts were still covered in his cum. Dried now, it held little appeal to him, but he knew he'd be spreading some over her again before long and called to Fred to come and help him. The man never looked at the woman, but helped him undress and then fisted his cock for him until he was hard again.

"Clean her up too. And with your tongue." The "yes sir" had Joel holding his own cock now as the manservant moved to the bed. He did just as he was told and lapped the dried cum off her breasts, then moved down her belly. Joel could see that she was wet, that whatever Fred was doing to her had her excited, but Joel let them play. It was almost as much fun to him as fucking was.

When she moaned, Joel took his place between her thighs. He wasn't ready to fuck her just yet, and was content to watch her being eaten by Fred. The man had a wonderful tongue, as Joel knew first hand. And when he freed his own cock, Joel watched him.

"You want to fuck her?" Fred said that he did. "You know what you'll have to do if I let you. You know how to repay me for letting you."

"I do, my lord." Fred had a lovely cock too. It was thick and hard, glistening at the end so that Joel was hard pressed not to take him into his mouth instead of letting him fuck the woman. "What would you like for me to do?"

Joel wanted it all. He wanted to be fucked by Fred, fuck the woman, and have his cock sucked too. He was a greedy man, but also knew that the drugs to keep him this hard were soon to wear off, and he wasn't going to be able to take any more until tomorrow. So he told Fred to have the woman, and he moved up behind the man to take him as well.

It was over quickly...at least his part was. He came almost as soon as he entered the tight hole on his manservant, but lingered long after Fred fucked the woman. Fred had the woman coming four times before he finally released, and Joel watched him as he pulled his clothing back on and left him with the woman.

She was nearly purring with her sexual releases. Joel only watched her as she laid there, her body still spread out before him like a feast; a feast that he was sick of looking at. He pulled out the knife that was in the nightstand and cut her lose. Then he told her to get out. Joel left the room a few minutes later to enter his own.

Joel took a shower, scrubbing off all the sex he'd had with them as hard as he could. Not that he was trying to wash away the enjoyment, but the smell of sex made him ill. It was why he never had it in his bedroom. And only with his servants. The woman, of course, would be gone tomorrow, her pocket full of cash and a reference in her hand. That was why he only hired women to service him and not clean his home. They were only useful for that one thing as far as he was concerned. And once his little pill wore off, he was finished with them all together.

"Oh Addison, where the fuck are you?" He was pissed every time he thought of her. She'd left him. And as much as he wanted to say good riddance to her, it was the fact that she'd left him without his permission that pissed him off the most. He didn't care for her any more than, he supposed, she did him, but he'd been promised her as his wife and, by God, she was going to be his wife. Even if in name only.

For five years she'd been gone. He had not a clue as to where she'd gone and not a hint of where she was staying, and even less of an idea as to how she was living. Joel had strongly believed that she was living in the mansion that her grandmother lived in. But his spies, people that he'd paid off to search, had never found so much as a note from her. And they had looked too, or so they'd told him just after they'd been found out by Mrs. Simon-English.

He had to find Addison. Now it was no longer a marriage that he wanted from her, a marriage that he didn't really care for, but he needed her to inherit his mother's money. No wife, no money, she'd told him. Where she'd gotten the idea that she could make the rules had surprised him, but he found out through a servant of his mother's that she'd been having visitors. Another reason to hate the fucking old bat.

Mrs. Simon-English had told his mother that requiring him to get married was the only way to ensure that she became a grandmother before her death. He had to talk to that fucking old bat too about staying out of his business. His mother wouldn't be making any more demands either, once he had Addison bowing before him. He'd see to that quick enough. But for now...well, for now he was sort of between a rock and a hard place.

"Like I want a child." Shuddering, he dressed with care, not waiting for Fred to come and assist him. "A sniffling, nasty, dirty child is not anything I want near me."

As he left his home, he told Fred that he'd be back in a week. It was time he did his own search of the Simon-English home, and there had better be some answers around for him to find. Then he was going to visit some of his mother's estates. She had several that he used on occasion, and he needed to relax before tackling Mrs. Simon-English, the old bitch herself. He wanted his mother's money almost as much as he wanted the West fortune. Joel Delaney was going to have it all.

~~~

Steele was sitting at the table enjoying some much needed down time and a nice hot cup of tea when someone came into the room. Ignoring him would have been easy, he supposed. He wasn't really there, but this man looked as confused as any ghost he'd ever met. And the man had been hurt...tortured badly before he'd been killed. Steele could see that as well. When the ghost wandered around the kitchen for the second time, Steele sighed. Then he looked at Nick when he entered the room and sat at the table. He, of course, could not see the ghost just yet.

"I was thinking about taking a drive around the city for a few days. Do you think you can spare me? I need...I just need to be gone for a while." Steele nodded to the ghost, and Nick looked in that direction. "Someone need you?"

"I would think he needs us both by the looks of him. Someone has taken a knife to his entire body and then shot him." The ghost looked at him and then looked at his body. "I don't think he knows just yet."

Ghosts, for the most part, were harmless. Especially the ones that came to see him. He had rules and, as he was very well known in the spectra world, those rules were seldom not followed. This man was here on his own, but Steele would bet from the look of this guy there would be more just like him.

"I think something happened to me." Steele told him he was sure of it. "I was...am I dead? I mean, how can I be walking around like this and not be?"

"I'm sorry to tell you, but you are. What is the last thing you remember?" The man sobbed and Steele waited. He knew that in a few minutes he'd have to tell the man he was dead again. It was as hard for them to realize that part of their demise as it was for someone being told they had a terminal disease.

"We were...there was a woman. She took us out of our home and...my wife? Have you found her yet?" Steele said that he'd not. "We were there with our family. In our house for the holidays. I think she might have killed us all. My wife and I were in the kitchen having a late...what happened to me?"

"You were murdered. What year was this, do you remember?" The man cried again but told him the year. Steele noticed that Nick was taking notes. "You've not been gone long, sir. Just about five months. Do you know what your name is?"

"My lovely wife. She was just sitting there and bam, that thing hit her in the head. The woman was with my oldest son. I told my wife that he didn't look like he was sure about them, but you know how the young are." Steele nodded and repeated everything to Nick. "She said—the woman, not my lovely wife—she said that she wanted to talk to us. Then she hit my wife. Margaret was her name. My Maggie. The woman's name was.... I'm sorry. I can't remember right now."

"That's fine. You're doing just fine. We're going to find you. And your family." Nick nodded and left them, only to return a few seconds later with a laptop. "Your name is...?"

"Charlie. Charles and Margaret Hicks." Nick was clicking away on the keyboard as Charlie continued. "My son is Charles too, but he never liked it. So he went by Sam, our middle name."

"Did you live in Ohio, Mr. Hicks?" Nick couldn't see the man, but he could ask him questions. "I have a missing report on Charles...I have a missing report."

When Steele looked at the computer as Nick turned it to him, he felt his heart twist. There was a list of names on the missing report that would keep them busy for a while. Charlie said he did live there and asked again what had happened to him.

"You've been killed by a woman who entered your home. What can you tell me about her? Anything? Like, do you remember what she looked like? What she sounded like?" Charlie said he couldn't remember and cried softly. "We'll find you, Charlie. If you can take me to where you woke up now, I'll have someone find the rest of your family too."

"She was his date. Sam had been single for a few years, his wife passing and leaving him with our granddaughter. Meggie, too, after her grandmother." Charlie cried harder. "She's dead too, isn't she? My little granddaughter, who never hurt nobody, is dead too."

Steele looked at the list and nodded, telling him that she was missing as well. He waited until Charlie could talk again before he asked him where he had come from. By the time he had some information to go on, the rest of the men in the house were up as well and joining them. Kari was helping to get breakfast on the table with their cook Izzy and her husband Jake.

Ray was making arrangements to go by van. They would all load into it, but Steele and Kari would go by car. Not that they would normally be separated from the group, but Charlie knew where he had been but not the address. He would have to follow the man by car as he made his way back to where his body had been tossed, no doubt. It was going to be a long day if the list that was on the missing report was any kind of indication.

It took them nearly an hour to find the gravesite. And by the time they'd called in the local police, the news vans had started to show up. It took Steele having to call in a favor to keep their names out of the paper, and no one was happy when the Feds showed up. It was a missing person's case up until the first body was discovered. Ray Hancock stood near him as the second, then the third body was found.

"You know how many are here?" Steele told him there might be as many as eleven. "Christ. Children too?"

"Yes." Ray hated it when children were involved. Well, to be honest, they all did. But when Aster came to stand next to him, he told her to go to Kari. She was taking this very hard. The little girl, Meggie, had found his wife, and Kari had never had to help with a child before this. Steele continued speaking with Ray as his sister went to his wife. "They were at his home for Christmas. The woman who killed them was with the son. He seemed confused, his dad said."

"You think she went there just to murder them?" Steele nodded. "Why? I mean, maybe she had a breakdown and just killed them on a whim."

"She tortured them. Charlie looks like she cut him up over a long period of time. I'm betting that the autopsy will show that they were all done the same way. She brought them here, but I don't think this is where they were killed. Charlie said he lived in this area, but this isn't his land."

"So we have to figure out where that is as well, unless it was his house. You think that's where she killed them?" Steele just stared at him. "You know, don't you? You know either who she is or where she is."

"I know who she is, but you're not going to like it." Ray started cursing, and Steele just smiled. "Yeah, I know what you mean. We tried to tell them when they released her that this would happen again."

Ellen Wooten had been in an institute for the criminally insane since she'd been eight. Ellie, as everyone had called her, had murdered not just her family, but the neighbors on both sides of them, as well as all the animals that had been in the houses. There were nineteen people killed and torn up by the child, and she'd been put away. Not her face, her name…nothing about her had hit the papers for over fifteen years, until about a year ago when her time served had been up and she'd been labeled as fit to return to society. A mistake by the system that was now coming back to haunt them in the worst kind of way.

"'Model patient,' they said. 'Never even raises her voice,' they said to me. I told them this would happen. I told them every day that fucking meeting was going on this would happen. Once those kind get a taste for it, there isn't a damned thing going to stop them." Steele let Ray go on. At least his voice was down so that the papers and news crews weren't getting any of it. "What the fuck are they going to do now? I ask you this."

"We find her, or help to find her, and have her put away again." They looked at the dogs going over the property, and Steele watched as they pulled out another body, this one wrapped in what looked to him like wrapping paper. "I know that it won't help these people, but we can hopefully save a few more."

It took them nearly nine hours to find them all. All the people on the missing list had been accounted for, and even the dog and cat that had been in the family had been found with the bodies, as if she'd wanted to keep them together for some reason. Steele was thinking how she would have needed plenty of time to dig these graves for them, not to mention bringing them all to this site. He wondered if she'd had any help, and decided to go and ask the group of ghosts that were gathered around each other.

"No. Not that we remember seeing." The little girl was standing next to who Steele assumed was her mom when Charlie answered him. "Suppose she could have when she...after she was done, but didn't see nobody that night."

"If you'd let me touch one of you, the way you are now, maybe I can get something more. Perhaps she left behind something on you that will let me see more of what happened to you all." Charlie put out his hand, but Steele shook his head. "I'm sorry, but not you. You've been...you've been dealing with this for too long. I need someone who is still unsure what has happened."

It had to be the child. He could see that she was still not understanding what had happened to her. Yes, she could see that her family was all hurt, but it hadn't occurred to her that all of them were as dead as she was. Steele knelt before her, careful not to frighten her.

When she shied behind her mom, Aster told him to let her do it. He watched his sister, someone that had been gone longer than this little girl had been alive, and let her take over for him. Her smile was as beautiful now as it had been the morning she'd left him and been killed.

"My name is Aster Bennett. Your name is Meggie, right?" The little girl nodded but didn't move from her mom. "I'm sure this is all very scary to you. It was when it happened to me, so I know all about being afraid. But my brother can help you all. Would you let him?"

"She hurt me. I didn't do anything wrong, but she still hurt me." Aster nodded and Steele knew that this was

16

costing his sister. She loved children as much as she had life. Her love of them had been what had gotten her killed that day. A simple act of kindness had led her into the path of a semi, and she'd been killed just like that. "I don't want anybody to hurt me again."

"And they never will, honey. Not ever again." Steele felt a hand on his shoulder and looked up at Kari. She could see as much as he could, but not the injuries. His wife was a necro as well, but not as strong as him. No one was as strong as he was. "My brother is going to help find that bad woman and make sure that she never hurts anyone again. But you have to let him touch just a part of you. I swear to you, it won't hurt you one bit."

The little girl stared at him, then looked up at her mom. The woman had suffered greatly at the hands of Ellen; not just her body, but her face as well. It was the same for the other family members that Ellen had killed. The women of the household had suffered the most.

"He won't hurt me?" Aster assured her that he wouldn't, not for anything. "And he'll catch her? She hurt my doggie too. I love Shep, and he needs to be taken to the hospital soon."

Steele only moved forward when little Meggie did. She was terrified, he could see that, but she was brave too, and he told her that. His touch to her cheek was just to assure her that he'd not hurt her, but he got more than he'd bargained for. The little girl had seen it all, her entire family being killed, before she was murdered too.

CHAPTER 2

Addie watched the men in the house. They were bringing in more and more equipment all the time. And the woman who was with them seemed to be in charge, but the guys didn't seem to realize it, not yet at least. Addie thought the woman was a great deal like Joel in that she simply expected you to do as she wanted, and fuck your opinion. He'd been like that with her every time she'd spoken to him.

Joel had told her right after her father had told her that she was marrying him what he expected of her as his wife. She had only sat there listening to him because it never occurred to her that he was serious. All she could think of was he was having fun with her. Something she would never have guessed he'd be doing, because as far as Addie knew, Joel didn't have a funny bone in his body. But she learned quickly enough that he was not only serious in his rules, but he wasn't going to let her have any say in anything, or she'd feel his wrath.

The slap had taken her breath away...not that she'd never been slapped before. Her father would hit her just because he felt that, while he'd not heard that she'd done anything wrong, it was his duty to make sure that she never did. But Joel had hit her when she'd spoken, as he said, out of turn.

"You will obey me, Addison. There will be no more of this temper of yours when we are wed. I simply won't tolerate it." She just stared at him with her hand on her cheek. "And don't think that tears will move me. There won't be any little bobbles or gifts to appease you either. I'm not going to apologize for keeping you in line, ever. When you mess up, I'm going to be swift in showing you how you've done so, and expect you to never mention it again. To anyone."

"You mean my grandmother." He drew back to hit her again and she stood up. One thing she'd learned that day...he hated that she was taller than him. "You touch me again, and so help me I will take you down."

It didn't matter what she said. He hit her again, over and over until she could no longer see straight. But she'd gotten in a few licks of her own...a kick to the groin, a chair over his head. She might have even gotten away from him had her father not chosen that moment to come and check on them. His hit had knocked her out.

Two days later it was in the paper that she was to wed Joel Delaney, and no amount of talking to the paper to get them to retract it or begging her parents would change any of that. She was fucked. And the fact that her grandmother was out of the country at the time this all was arranged had not helped her one bit. Three days before her birthday, her grandmother had returned, and with her, a hell like no other had ever seen.

"You love him?" Addie told her not only did she not love him, but that she loathed him, and her grandmother had nodded. "I've talked to your father. A stupider man I've never known. He won't budge either. And I told my daughter that I was done with her too. You know what she said to me? 'One gets used to it after a while.' She's as dumb as he is, I think." Addie laughed, but it was short lived as well when she realized she had nowhere to turn.

"I won't marry him." Grandmother nodded. "I mean...I just won't. He told me that I'd never see you again either, even if he had to have you committed and then killed to keep us apart."

"We'll see about that. I've been around a good deal longer than that little pisser, and I plan to be around a good deal longer." Her grandmother put her hand on Addie's chin. "Did he do this?"

"Yes." Grandmother nodded but didn't say any more. "He's going to do it again if he finds out that I'm here. And you should see the guards that he has on me when I go out. May has been fired too. I've known her my entire life, and now he has this woman that he's picked out to take care of my needs. I don't have any needs that she can take care of...she wants to dress and undress me. Fuck that crap."

"He is old school for such a young millionaire. And a moron." Grandmother dismissed the woman in the corner of the room with them. She didn't want to go, but Grandmother got what she wanted even if she had to use force. Bentley, her best friend and butler, had forced the woman out of the room bodily when she wouldn't go. "This will cost you too, I would imagine. So you have to think quickly and move on it. But don't tell me. I don't...when you go, just call me to tell me you're gone so I know that no one murdered you."

When she handed her a card with a number on the back, Addie had had a feeling it was going to help her. Her grandmother had kissed her on the cheek and held her just a little longer than she normally would have before telling her how much she loved her. Addie had a feeling that her grandmother knew that her days within this house were numbered too.

Going to the bank the morning of her birthday had been difficult, and she might not have been able to pull it off had the clerk in the wedding shop not been on her grandmother's payroll. As soon as she was put into a room to try on the dress that Joel had picked out for her to wed him in, Addie was shown to the back of the place, where a cab was waiting for her. When Addie asked the woman if she'd be all right, she told her that she was going to be if Addie got away. Smiling, she handed Addie a letter from her grandmother and told her to go to the bank. It was arranged there too.

The sound of screaming had Addie going to her little window that looked out over the yard. The barn wasn't as bad as she'd first thought, and it afforded her a perfect view of the yard and front door to the house.

Addie had been living in the house until a few days ago when a couple of men had shown up. They were talking about bringing back some equipment and some ghost hunting items to the house. Addie still found it hard to believe that anyone would be stupid enough to think that dead people wandered around like they showed you in the movies.

The man stumbling out of the house covered in blood made her glad that she'd moved to the barn as soon as the men had left the first time, and not waited to see if they'd return. Addie stared at the macabre scene below her in a kind of horrific stupor.

Addie nearly screamed when the woman came out behind him with what appeared to be a large sword in her hands. When the woman grabbed the man's hair, Addie thought for sure that she was seeing if he was all right, but soon saw that she was wrong. His head was removed almost as soon as the woman got to him, and it tumbled across the yard to land looking up at her. Addie scrambled away from the window so quickly that she nearly fell off the short ledge.

Her heart was pounding so hard that she was sure that anyone going by the big barn could have heard it. When the door to the barn squeaked open, Addie moved with the utmost care. There was nowhere to hide up here, so she covered herself with the hay, hoping and praying that the woman wasn't coming to find her as well.

"Hello?" Addie whimpered a little but didn't move. The woman had seen her; that was all her mind could focus on right now. "Where are you? I know that you're in here. I could smell you all over the house. It never occurred to me that you'd still be around, but here you are."

Addie covered her mouth and nose with her shirt and closed her eyes as she tossed the hay over her. The creaking of the door didn't fool her one bit. The woman was still in here with her. Addie decided that she'd lay here for days before she gave in and moved, if that was all it took to keep her alive.

The ladder was being used. The sound of it scraping the edge of the loft, where she was, gave her reason to believe that she'd be dead within minutes. Her family—well, her grandmother—would never know what had happened to her. Joel would be madder still at her. A small giggle started to bubble up from her belly, and she only just managed to stifle it when the hay near her head moved.

"Did you see my handiwork?" The voice was very close to her, but Addie didn't move. "I killed Peter too. What a douche bag. Both of them really. They were going to find me out with their machines, and I just couldn't have that. I have a great deal of work yet I want to do. Well, not so much work, but playing. I so love to play."

A slicing sound had Addie holding her breath tighter within her. While she had no idea what it was, she knew as surely as she lay there that it would not bode well for her. As the noise echoed again, Addie knew what it was the moment that the pain in her arm caused her to be terrified. Not that she wasn't already. But the woman was slicing the knife into the hay around her, looking, no doubt, for her or anyone that was hiding up here.

"You never know about people, I guess. Here I thought that I was the only one that knew about this place, and then these assholes put an ad in the paper asking for an assistant. I applied—they told me that I was the only one really, but I had to see if they could do it. Never in a million years did I think that they would. But they thought they could, and who knew? They were able to record ghosts on their little machines." The noise was closer to her body now. Addie knew that something had cut her, and hoped that her blood wouldn't give her away. "I guess we'll never know now if what they found was just squiggly lines or a ghost that I had made the last time I was here. I got...I guess I got a little greedy in my need to draw more blood."

This time the pain centered in her right side. The pain was so great that Addie screamed silently behind her hand. Whatever the woman had stabbed into her, Addie knew that this time it was deep. In her pain, she thought of the man at the cemetery.

Oh, how I wish you were here now, Nicholas. The connection to him was profound. And even if she didn't actually know him, she felt comforted by him touching her mind. *I'm going to die this time, and without you being a part of it.*

Where are you? Smiling, the woman still talking above her, Addie told him that she had no idea but that she was in a barn. *What state? Do you know the city?*

After telling him what she could remember, he told her to wait for him. *Yeah, well, I have nowhere to go, so that isn't going to be hard. Will you contact my grandmother?*

What's her name? Addie didn't think she told him, just thought of the grief her grandmother would feel when she was dead. *I'll contact her. Who else? Anyone else that I need to notify for you?*

No. No one cares. But you can't tell Joel, Joel Delaney, about me. He's a monster of the worst kind. The woman said something, and Addie wanted to ask her what she'd said. Then as she moved by her, her foot stepping between her legs like she knew she was there, Addie talked to the man of her dreams. *I'm going to die. This woman was here with two men and she killed them. I don't know her name, but they were here to film ghosts of the dead. There are no such things as ghosts, and now because they're stupid, I'm going to die.*

You're not going to die, and there are ghosts. I'm coming, Addie. I'll be there soon. Just hang on for me. She told him she would try. *Just hang on for me.*

~~~

Nick told Mitch, who was riding with him, what Addie had told him. The car they were in lurched forward as Mitch pressed down on the gas pedal. If they got there, it would be faster than if Steele or any of the others were driving because, as much as he loved Mitch, he drove like a race car driver most of the time. Nick called Steele and told him what was going on just as he and Mitch pulled into the long drive of the house that Charlie had sent them to.

"It has to be the same house. I mean, how many houses do you think are in the middle of nowhere that she used to murder her victims?" Steele agreed with him and told him they were there already. "We're in the driveway. Go to the barn. She's in there."

"I'm there now. I don't see anything." Before the car was at a complete stop, Nick was jumping out and running to the barn. The men were in there, all of them, looking for Addie and calling her name. Nick closed his eyes and tried to reach for her again, but didn't feel her any longer. Something dripped on his face, and he rubbed it off and looked at Kari, who was in front of him.

"What?" When she looked up, he did as well. There was nothing there but an overhang and some straw or something hanging over the edge. "What is it you see?"

"You have blood on your face." Nick looked down at his hand, then at her. "She's up there somewhere. We just have to figure out how to get up there."

Steele found the ladder that had been taken off. It had blood on it as well, and Steele and Drew held it steady for Nick as he climbed up. He tried to judge where the blood had dripped onto his face and the place above it to find her. When he was at the top, he got off the ladder clumsily in his haste, and nearly fell to his death when he tripped. The straw under his foot was drenched in blood.

"I found her." Or at least he hoped so. Taking off the shirt that was over the woman's face, he looked down at Addie, his future wife. "She's stabbed, twice that I can see. Pulse is weak. And she's lost a great deal of blood."

The medics that were there with them made their way up the ladder much as he had, carefully and quickly. As soon as he was asked to move back, Nick started to tell them her name when they asked, but stopped himself. He had to keep her identity a secret, as well as the fact that she was alive.

Steele was coming up the ladder when Nick started to fall apart. One look from the man and Nick could feel his back start to stiffen up again, and he started to ask for things that he knew he should be caring for himself. But he didn't want to leave her. Not yet, at any rate. Steele seemed to know why he was doing it. Nick was scared shitless and didn't want anyone to mess this up for her. Or him for that matter. Steele only nodded and told him he was on it. Then Nick sat down hard on the hay.

"She saw her." Steele came the rest of the way up the ladder and sat beside him while the men worked. "She saw her, and now she might die before I get to know her."

"I'm sure she's in good hands." One of the medics turned to him and nodded. "See? Carl said she's going to be fine."

"Sure she is. We just have to flight her in. Where you want her? And the hospital will want some information on her. What you got for me?" Steele told him nothing for now. "Works for me. Jane Doe here will be just that, a nameless victim."

As soon as they were ready to transport, Nick stood up. He and Steele looked around the tiny area and found not just her clothing and a large duffle, but some food stashed as well. Steele tossed it down to Ray, who was near the car, and they put it in the trunk. Nick was going to the hospital with Addie, and the rest of them were going to work the scene. The police arrived just as the helicopter was dusting off the ground. No one said a word about Addie. Nick got in the front with the pilot and watched the guys in the back work their magic.

By the time they were at the hospital, they'd gotten her stabilized and had her prepped for surgery. Addie had asked him to do one thing, and he had to make the call before he saw her again.

It took him nearly an hour to figure out who to call, only because he'd called Steele again and asked him if he knew anyone there. A quick trip by Billy to the home had given them not just the phone number, but a person to ask for. Nick didn't think asking to speak to Mrs. English would get him very far.

"Hello, I need to speak to Bentley, Don Bentley please." The woman who answered the phone in the kitchen told him to hang on. It sounded like an argument was going on close by, and Nick tried to get as much information as he could before someone came back on the line. "He wants to know what you want. There's something…that man is back, and the missus is working on getting him out of the house before we have to call the police on him again."

Nick had no idea who she was talking about, and really didn't care right now. What he had to do was think of some way to get a message to Addie's grandmother. What could he tell Mr. Bentley so the man wouldn't think he was scamming him? "Tell him that I need to speak with Mrs. English. I have some…four million, seven hundred thousand questions for him." It was the amount of money in the second bag that they'd found with Addie. The phone was put down again, and within seconds a different woman came back.

"Who is this?" Nick told her who he was. "That means nothing to me, young man. What do you know about that kind of money?"

"Mrs. English?" He was corrected on her name. "And so you know, I never said that was a money amount. I just told you I had that many questions to ask you, that's all."

There was silence at the other end for so long that Nick thought for sure she'd hung up on him. If it hadn't been for the loud voices in the background, he might have believed it. But when the sound was cut off abruptly, he knew that she'd either gone to another part of the house or had put everyone out of the kitchen.

"Is she all right?" He told her that she'd been stabbed multiple times but was in stable condition for now. "I can't come to her. If I do then he'll come for her too. I...I need to know that she's in good hands, Mr. Stark. She's all I have."

"You mean Joel Delaney." She told him that was right. "Addie told me that he is the worst kind of monster and I wasn't to tell him where she is. But she's in good hands. No one knows who she is but me and the men I work with, and I trust them with my life. Hers too."

"I'm going to give you a number to call me on. I want you to use it no matter the time. The man who will answer, his name is Bentley. How you got his name in all this is beyond me, but you scared him. Bentley is a very cautious man, and you did well in making him nervous. I'd like to know how you did that sometime." He told her it would be his pleasure to tell her.

After he got the number she hung up on him. Nick didn't know if she was afraid her phone was bugged or not, but the call could already have been traced. A few minutes later a nurse at the desk told him he had a call. Nick took it, thinking it was Steele or one of the others.

"Move her. Now." It was all the man said before the line went dead. Nick handed the phone back to the nurse and called Steele using his personal cell phone. He told him what had happened and who he'd talked to, ending with the man telling him he had to move her.

"I'll make some arrangements. Tell no one. I don't know what's going on, but we'll get her out within the hour." Steele could move mountains with the kind of money he had, and Nick knew that. "Don't be alarmed if a few of our friends show up. They're going to help you. Carlton is in charge and...Christ, I can't believe I'm saying this, but he has an idea to get her out and I trust him."

"If you do, then...he's here now. I'll call you back." Nick looked at Carlton and Donny. If there was ever a more mismatched pair of friends, Nick wasn't sure he'd want to meet them. "She's in surgery still. What do you want me to do?"

"Nothing. That way if it comes out, you're a free and clear guy." Donny laughed. "She a looker? I could use a nice looking girl for my upcoming vid."

"You stay away from her. People are looking for her." Donny nodded. "But seriously, what are you going to do?"

Carlton told him to just sit there and be a good boy. "We are going to get her out of here with the help of some of our friends that have passed on as we have. They will...never you mind, young man. Just suffice it to say that there will be a great distraction while we move. Once she's outside, there will be a van waiting for her, and then we'll take her to the big house. Steele is hiring a good doctor to come in and keep an eye on her for you. After that, young man, we're going to be fine. And so will she."

Nick had no idea what the plan was, and a huge part of him thought that was a good idea. However, it didn't lessen his fear on it all falling apart. Carlton was old, like centuries old, and Donny was just a kid...one that had been around for a while, but still only a kid.

About ten minutes later a doctor came down the hall. Nick watched the man walking and it looked to him like he was drunk. But the closer he got, the more he realized the man was confused. As he sat down after asking Nick if he was with the Jane Doe, he looked at him with dazed eyes.

"She's just gone. I mean…we brought her out and the nurses started screaming. I went to look and…and she was gone." Nick asked him who was gone, because there was no way the ghosts could have pulled this plan off that quickly. "The Jane Doe. The nurses said…well, never mind what they said they saw, but when I went back to the room where she was being transported into to recover, I just…I thought for sure that…something is very wrong here."

"You've lost a patient?" He almost felt sorry for the man. He really was upset about this. "I'm sure you can call the police and have them come in and look. Or perhaps she was taken to another floor. Did you check on that?"

"No. I don't…maybe. But I don't think so. And the things that we saw." He looked at him and his body shuddered. "There was a man coming at me with his head in his hand. And he was asking me to fix it back on for him. And the woman? Christ, she was carrying her arm in her hand too, but she was using it to wave at us all when she saw someone…. Just holding onto it like one would a child. She smiled at me, and I swear to God there was a huge bug lying there instead of her tongue."

Nick could see them doing that. It was all he could do not to laugh. He would bet he knew each of the ghosts that the doctor described, and would have to thank them for helping. Old ghosts could make themselves known to the living, but it would cost them if they hadn't been summoned previously by the living. Nick would bet it was the most fun these people had had in decades.

"I don't think I'd tell the police that if I were you." The doctor said he wasn't going to. "Also, maybe...I don't know...perhaps you can just forget about the woman too. Maybe...maybe we've both been...punked. Perhaps she wasn't hurt at all. And it was a joke on us."

"You think?" He sounded so hopeful that Nick nodded. "I think you might be right. That wound in her belly didn't look that bad. Maybe it wasn't. Perhaps...I think you might be right there, young man. I'm going to go and talk to my staff right now and tell them that. The nerve of some people. What if someone with a true injury came in needing me and she had us all tied up?"

By the time he left Nick, the doctor was no longer hazy about the events, but he was pissed off. The dazed and confused look on his face was gone now and he looked determined. Nick left too. As soon as he was out of the building, Carlton met him in the parking lot with Donny.

"You did a good job." Bowing at the waist, Carlton smiled at him. "The guy with his head off and the woman...do you know them, or were they just hanging around here waiting to help you? Because I'd very much like to thank them personally."

"I knew him in the French war. The man had been beheaded for stealing, and could never bring himself to go with his beloved. I think we gave him the courage to go on." They both looked at Donny when he wolf whistled. "That young man should have a leash. I found him in the nurses' lounge just a bit ago watching them put on their work uniforms. I wonder, were you that bad at twelve?"

"No. My stepfather and mother wouldn't have allowed me to have any fun like that." Carlton told him he was sorry to have brought it up. "No worries, my friend. You know my dad."

"I do indeed. And you know that he is looking for you?" Nick told him that he knew and wasn't worried. "If you need me, you know that I am here for you, young Nick. And the young woman. She is a beautiful woman, if you don't mind my saying."

"Thanks." He went to the car that had been sent for him and got in the back. Knowing Steele did have a lot of nice perks. This one, riding in the back of the limo, gave him time to think and to plan.

Nick hoped that Addie was all right. This was way beyond anything he'd ever done before...for the living or the dead. And if this Joel person was as bad as Addie said he was, there was something else to consider. She might be a target for two people instead of just the one. And Ellen Wooten was bad enough.

CHAPTER 3

"Lady Evie, that man is here to see you again. I thought yesterday was going to be the end of Mr. Delaney." Evie rolled her eyes at her butler. "I have tried to put him off, but he is insistent that he speak with you. He has questions about Miss Addie. I have asked him to wait out of doors for you. That did not go over well, as you can imagine."

"I'm sure that it didn't. Let me go to the parlor and when I'm settled, you bring him in. And please stay with me. I don't want to kill the man and have to go to jail for it. I have no idea why he's still trying to find my Addie after all this time. Do you? The man is a fool if you ask me." Bentley shook his head and smiled at her. "You're up to something. What is it?"

"You have heard that she is all right and it shows on your face. It makes you feel better, doesn't it?" It did too. Hearing from that young man yesterday had made her do a little dance in the kitchen. Then she'd had Bentley call him back and tell him to get her out of the place she was in. There were ears everywhere in her house, and she'd not have Addie hurt because of Delaney and his misguided attempts at getting her back. "Shall I have tea for the two of you, or will he not be here that long?"

"We'll let him hang himself today. But I swear to you, should he get on my nerves today, I won't be responsible for what happens. Have you heard from that man at his place? Fred Snyder?" Bentley flushed, and she smiled at him. "I'm an old woman, Bentley, and have heard a little about men."

"Mr. Delaney has had sex with him recently. Fred is...he is becoming very sick of the man and wishes to leave his employment. The women are fine, he says, but not Delaney. What shall we do?" Evie wasn't surprised to hear that about Delaney. The man was sick and had to take drugs too. She knew a great deal about the man that no one else was privy to. "He wishes to quit, and I can't say that I blame him."

"Send a car for him. Tell him to meet the car at...I don't know, you arrange that part. Have him go to the house in Paris. He should be safe there until this is over. The butler there passed on a few weeks ago, and I've not even looked into replacing him." Bentley told her he'd take care of it as soon as Mr. Delaney left. "No. Now. He can cool his heels. I just wish it was raining on his sorry ass."

Ten minutes later Fred had his arrangements set and Evie was in her parlor. A wooden tea trolley had been set up, and the camera's that had been set up in this room without her permission were staring right at her. She was going to take care of those too when Joel left. The nerve of the little pisser to spy on her. Soon, she kept telling herself. Soon she'd be talking face to face with her little Addie.

"Mrs. English-Simon. I thought you'd forgotten about me." She told him she'd tried, but he kept coming back. "I wish I knew why you disliked me so much. Whatever have I done to you? We're going to be related by marriage as soon as I find—"

"Cut the shit, Delaney. I don't dislike you at all. I loathe you. What do you want? And if this is about my Addie, then you're wasting your time. Again. I've told you that I don't know where she is, and nothing has changed since yesterday." He sat down and leaned against the back of her sofa like he owned the place. "What do you want now?"

"I've come to ask you again where you have her hidden. And I will continue to do so until I get her back where she belongs. I know that you have something to do with her being gone. I don't know how yet, but I'll find out. And when I do, there will be hell to pay. By both of you." She only stared at him and sipped her tea. "She's going to be my wife. Come hell or high water, I'm going to marry her and then fuck her. You should know that I always get what I want."

"Do you?" Evie looked at Bentley, and he nodded to her. "Do you really? And the woman you wanted several weeks ago? Did you get her? Or the man from three nights ago? Did he come to you willingly, or did you have to pay him after you raped him in the back of your limo?"

Delaney paled and sat up straighter on the couch when Bentley handed him a thick file, filled with all sorts of photos...all of them of Delaney and all of them with him and some other person in a compromising position. She could have had recording devices planted too if she wanted, but preferred the old fashioned method of cameras. For now at least.

"Where did you get these?" She noticed that he didn't deny any of them, but stared at a few like he was memorizing them or something. "This one shows my best side. I'd like to have a copy of this one, if you don't mind. But as far as forcing anyone? No, I didn't have to. And you won't be able to prove it even if I did."

She knew the moment that he found the letter from the woman in the pictures. It was a signed document that stated that not only had Delaney raped her, but had given her cash to keep her from going to the police. The money that he'd given her was there as well, all five grand of it.

"That poor girl is not going to be easy for you to find, Delaney. I've taken her under my wing and she's going to be safe until such time as I can have you taken care of." He asked her what that was supposed to mean. "And you might need to find another bed partner in the way of a butler. Mr. Snyder has left your employment as well. Poor man couldn't take it any longer."

"Who?" She told him who the man was. "Fred won't leave me. I have enough dirt on him to keep him under lock and key for a good long time."

Evie sipped her tea and then ate a scone while he stared at her. She wasn't worried. Fred was on her private plane right now. The man was so happy to be gone from the house that he'd left immediately, and when he'd been picked up by her car, her driver said he was dancing. He, too, would sign a document telling all that he knew about the man in front of her.

"So you've had a spy in my home. Not very nice of you." She nodded to the camera that was hidden in one of the vases in this room. A crew would be going over the rest of the house today, but his visit was going to bring them in now. "As for Fred? I was getting tired of him anyway, so good riddance to him. But I'm not here to compare how much we're keeping an eye on each other. I want you to tell me where Addison is. It's well past time that she became the new Mrs. Delaney. And I mean now, Evie. I'm not fucking around any longer."

"It's funny you should mention the new Mrs. Delaney. I've been looking for the other two wives of yours. Where are they, Delaney?" He only smiled at her. "I've found Sheila. Poor thing was no happier in the institute than Fred was with your company. She's much better off and less drugged up than she's been since you put her away. Couldn't kill her, could you?"

"So? I've been married before. What difference does that make?" But she could tell that he was nervous about it. "How many times have you been married?"

"Twice. Both of them I outlived. And I would say being married five times and widowed four is bad odds, and not in my granddaughter's favor, wouldn't you? What did you do to them? Or should I be asking you what do you think they did to you that you had to resort to murder to have them gone?" He stood up then and walked the short distance between them. Bentley was there before he could get within a foot of her.

"You're going to back the fuck off right now, Evie. Or so help me, you'll suffer in ways that you never have before."

She stood up too, and Delaney drew back his fist. She had no idea if he was going to hit her or just threaten her, but he seemed to fall backwards all on his own and landed on the trolley. The sliver of wood coming out of his neck had him grabbing it and trying to stop the blood. For a whole second, no longer, she thought about just watching the blood drain from him, but couldn't do it. She wasn't going to help him, but she wasn't going to watch him die.

"Call the police, Bentley. I believe that Mr. Delaney has had an accident." Bentley moved to the phone in the room, and Evie stared down at Joel. "You stupid, foolish man. What am I going to do now? I do suppose that Addie will be safe with you dead. But to tell the truth, I have no idea where she is."

By the time the police arrived, Delaney, of course, was dead. She told them about the camera in the room and that she had no idea where it was. But a quick call to Fred on his way out of the country told them all they needed to know. She was left with a stain on her carpet and a relief so profound that she giggled. Of course, not until after they'd all left them alone. Addie really was safe, and Evie was happier than she'd been in a long time.

~~~

Ellen moved around the house and decided while it wasn't nearly as perfect as the one from before, she could play here. It sat far enough off the road that she could have as much fun as she wanted, and there was only one way onto the property with the fast moving river behind it. Ellen was so happy that she decided to let the woman showing her around the place live. At least for now.

"I'll take it. You say that I can rent it on a month to month lease until they sell?" The woman nodded and told her that as soon as it sold she'd have ninety days to move out, less if the new owners wanted to take it now. "I'll bet it's been on the market for a while, right?"

"I'm sorry to say that it has been. Nearly four years. The market just isn't what it used to be. Houses like this one, with all this property, usually get bought up by a big company and then ravaged to make room for condos. But there is very little appeal for a house in this area, even if it is cheap. And while I hate to mention this, there is very little in the way of cable or Internet services out here. Nothing to do for the young urbanites, I guess."

Ellen didn't know what that meant, but nodded. She had missed a great deal being in a home for so long, and she'd had to be so good too. That meant that she'd not talked to a great many people, and those that she did, Ellen had to refrain from killing them by keeping her distance as much as she could. That was the hardest part. Not killing everything that breathed.

The house was much smaller than she'd thought to live in. But everything else about the place appealed to her more than the size of the house. All she could think about was the other house, the one that she'd killed the two men in. It had everything, including the barn. Ellen loved barns. Her first bodies had been in a barn. Then her daddy had caught her, and that had been the end of that area for her.

Setting up the home so that she could live there while she looked for some of her next victims, her mind kept going back to the other house. She was sure that the police had removed the other two men by now and cleaned up after her. Ellen thought that whoever had been in the barn, if there had been anyone, was long gone too. But the van pulling into the yard just as she was leaving had startled her enough that she'd left unfulfilled about the killings. She'd not been able to play with them. Something that had kept her sane for years was the thought of getting to play for as long as she wanted when she got out.

This house had been recently cleaned, the realtor told her. The carpets had been steam cleaned and fresh paint was on the walls. Ellen missed the pink in the bathroom that she'd used the one time she'd been at the other house, and the small towels, while dusty, which had been hanging on the towel holder in the bath. The guys had complained about the appliances in the kitchen, but those too had given her a great joy. Ellen thought that she'd go back there just to play one more time, just to break the house in all by herself.

Going up to the furnished bedroom, she lay down on the small bed.

Ellen thought of the week she'd had before they locked her up. That had been the best time of her life. Even the small animals that she'd caught sometimes and killed had not given her the thrill that killing all those people did when she was a kid.

Her parents had been the first she killed, of course, and they might have lived had her mother not been a harpy. Christ, when she thought of how much they had bossed her around, she wished that she could find them and do it all over. But killing them had helped her to do a better job of the Jeffersons, who lived on one side of them. Then the Weeks, who had lived on the other. By the time the police had shown up, she had mastered it to the point where she'd been perfect.

A killing machine was how she thought of herself. And she'd done so well with the old couple and their family when she'd first gotten out of the home that she could not wait to do it again and again. They were just the first of many. Ellen didn't count the two men she'd killed. There had been no time to play, and she knew that was what had counted most to her.

On one of the days leading up to Ellen being caught, her mom had been making some kind of dessert that she was going to take to a function at work the next morning. But her mouth had never shut up. She was forever complaining about how Ellie—as they'd called her back then—was dressed, how her hair looked, and how she wore mismatched socks. The knife was in Ellen's hand and sticking out of her mother's mouth before she could think that she shouldn't do this in the house, but it was too late by then. After that, it had been a blood bath for her. And so much fun.

Elaine Wooten had died much too quickly for Ellen's tastes. Of course, Ellen had watched the blood pour in great buckets, it seemed, from the back of her mother's throat. As it pooled beneath her, Ellen picked up another knife from the big block on the counter and began stabbing her mom in the belly and arms. Blood had squirted all over her unmatched socks and stringy hair as she brought the knife up and down over and over. Her dad, coming in to see what all the noise was about, she supposed, had her looking up at him and smiling.

"What have you done? Oh my God, you've killed your mother, Ellie! I can't cover this one up. I won't! Not this time." Ellen remembered looking down at her mom, thinking he was quite proud of her. "You've killed her, don't you realize that? What the hell is wrong with you?"

When he reached for the phone, she'd leapt at him. Her plan was only to stop him, but the knife had entered his belly just as he'd put his fingers on the handset. When he dropped to the floor, the knife still sticking out of him, Ellen realized that this was going to be great. She was going to watch them both die, and learn what she hadn't the first time she'd killed someone. It had been a mistake to let her father find the man before she'd been done.

Her dad lasted a little longer than her mom had. Not by a lot, but enough for Ellen to know that she had to do something more to make sure they would continue to beg her. That was what she'd enjoyed the most, she had figured out quickly...the way they pleaded with her to stop. Her dad had told her he'd give her anything should she just let him live. Ellen had all she wanted by then and told him so. Over and over. But soon there wasn't anyone to work on.

Her parents were dead, and she had gotten bored quickly with eating what she wanted and watching the porn stations on the television. It was not all that interesting, she remembered thinking. Taking a shower and putting on something clean, she made her way across the yard to the neighbors.

The next house that she'd entered was the Jefferson house. They just let her in when she told them that her parents had sent her over to see if they had any aspirin. Mrs. Jefferson had told her she'd get it for her, and Ellen asked to use the bathroom. It was how she'd gotten to the kids first.

They had six kids, but she'd had to kill them quickly. They whined and the sound of it, the high pitched noise of it, still made her angry when she realized they'd done it on purpose to piss her off. So much so that when she was in lock-up, she'd have to leave the room when one of the others would do it. It would set her on edge in no time.

Two had been in their bed, which made it quick and quiet. The other four, two in one room and two huddled in a closet, had been easy pickings for her. But the parents gave her more than enough to make up for having to kill their children so quickly.

Ellen took her time with them. With the blade of the knife at the husband's throat, she'd forced the wife to tie the male to the bed, then tied the woman down herself, threatening to kill her husband if she didn't cooperate. Ellen had gone from one to the other, just cutting into them to hear them beg. When Mrs. Jefferson started screaming, her voice a needle going through her head, Ellen had ended her after the second day in the house.

Mr. Jefferson had offered her everything, as her father had done, including money and his car. What he thought she'd do with either had been beyond her when he was so perfectly there for her now. As she cut into him, his guts hanging out of his body like a long cord, she'd had music playing in the background that made her feel like dancing. And she had, right there on the bloodied floor, while he told her what he was going to do with her when he was loose. Which of course, he never did.

Ellen had gone to her house after being with the Jefferson's for three days. They had played with her nicely at the Jefferson house, and now she was really ready to get down to perfecting her cutting. After cleaning herself up, washing her hair and even making sure that her socks matched, she walked to the only other house within miles and knocked on the door to the Weeks's house. She used the same ploy as before, asking for a bottle of aspirin for her mom. Little did they know she no longer had any use for the stuff.

As soon as she was let in, one of the boys rolled his eyes at her. Ellen closed the door, clicked the lock, and turned to him. Bart was dead before he was a few feet from her; she'd cut his throat open with the long machete she'd found in the Jefferson house. It was perfect for making quick work of assholes like Bart.

The car entering her drive pulled her from her thoughts. The man who got out of the car looked like he was lost, but she didn't move just yet. He was too close to his car for her to go out and take him, and he was big. Being in the home for so long had taught her that bigger didn't always mean meaner, but when there was a fight, it would always overpower. When he stepped up onto the little porch, Ellen picked up her small knife and went to the door. Fun time was going to be sooner than she'd thought.

The man was looking to his left when she opened the door. It was then that she saw the woman in the car. The woman was staring at them both like she was going to be drawing them later, and Ellen slid the knife back behind her. Too much could happen with the woman out in the car. And as much as she wanted to make this man her first in this house, she didn't need to try and kill him and chase down the car too. Ellen didn't know how to drive yet, and had no idea how to bring her back should she have been able to stop her from leaving.

"Hello. We're looking for June Stable. Do you…are you her?" Ellen shook her head and didn't say anything. "My wife and I are supposed to bring her some things. There was a death in her family recently, and the address we were given isn't showing up on our GPS."

"I just moved to this area. I don't know anyone." Ellen watched him with her fingers itching to take out the knife and kill him. "I'm sorry. You'll have to look elsewhere."

The man nodded and had started back for the car when he stopped and turned to look at her. Ellen felt as if he was trying to place her, but she knew that wasn't possible. She'd been gone a long time, and there was no way she'd have forgotten him if he worked at the home where she'd been.

"Do I know you? I know that's a weird thing to say, but you look like someone I should know." He turned back to her, staring at her like there was going to be a contest later. "I think I should know you, but I just can't place you. Funny, right?"

"Nope. Like I said, I just came to this area." He nodded and moved forward again, only to stop and stare at her. Ellen started to come out of the house and kill him anyway despite the woman, when he turned back to his car and hurried to it. He was peeling out of the drive even before she could take a step off the porch. She had no idea what was going on, but then heard something making a noise on the porch. The man had dropped something. As she bent to pick it up, it chirped again.

The cell phone was something that, while she was familiar with it, she had not had a lot of practice with. Some of the people at the home had them, of course, and used them a great deal, so she knew how they worked. But as far as knowing how to call someone, she wouldn't have had anyone to call anyway. Picking it up, she took it into the house and sat it on the table until it stopped making a screeching noise before she picked it up and inspected it.

It only took her a second to figure out how to open the screen up. There were a lot of little pictures too, mostly games on his phone. But when she started to close some of them up, hitting the little back arrow in the corner, she came across a picture of herself. It was one that they had taken of her the day that she'd been released.

It was an article, she thought. But since she didn't know how to use the thing, all she got was the headline. And that was more than enough to have her packing her few things and getting out of the house. "Wooten Murder Spree" with her picture next to it was going to bring a lot of people to her door, and very soon too.

It took her an hour to get out of the house. Just as she was moving out of the back door, the driveway was filling with police cars and a large dark van. The letters SWAT on the side had her frightened enough that she nearly fell over the bench in the back yard and bloodied her knee. Running to the woods, she was to them when she heard the front door crash open and men shouting. Ellen climbed the first tree she could get into and watched as they moved all around the yard.

The man in the car had called someone. Ellen just knew it. And now she had not only lost her home, but her place to play as well. When the sound of a helicopter flying over her head reached her ears, she stared up at it. This was a lot of manpower, was all she could think. There had to be a reason that she was suddenly being pursued. Surely there had to be something else, some other reason why they had a manhunt out for her. No one could have found out that she'd been playing again so soon.

It had been months since she'd killed, and that had been at the victims' house. Of course, there were the two men she'd killed, but again, she refused to count them, and would be really upset if the police tried to blame them on her. She had killed them, of course, but not the way she had wanted to. There were rules, and hers were they weren't murder unless she cut them. Which, of course, she hadn't had time to do. There had to be something else. Someone…. Ellen thought of the noise that she'd heard in the barn.

"Someone was up there." She knew that now. And as much as she'd looked around, the person had evaded her. Had she had more time…? "Well, that's going to have to be taken care of now. I don't know who it was, but there has to be some way I can find out."

As the men fanned out under her hiding place, Ellen tried to think what she had to do now. There was no way she could stay here, of course. She knew that they'd be looking for her harder too, and this house would be watched for a long time. Longer than she wanted to wait for them to leave her alone again. More than likely the other one too, but that was where she wanted to be. Deciding to go back to the house with the pretty green shutters and ugly green appliances, Ellen waited until dark before jumping down from the tree and making her way back to the house.

She'd have to walk it. Hitching a ride was going to be out of the question now, but she'd get there. And when she did, she'd be making sure that no one got the jump on her again. Ellen was going to make sure of that. There was no way, not ever, she was going back to that home.

Walking with her pack of things, Ellen thought of all the things she was going to have to do to set up again. She was glad that whoever had told on her at the house hadn't waited until she had things just the way she'd wanted them, or she would have had to leave her toys behind. Ellen so loved her toys. Anything sharp wouldn't do. It had to call to her. Sort of make her feel like they were meant to be together. She supposed in some way that was what it was. Her toys were as drawn to her as she was to them. And she'd had no problem stealing them when they did call out to her.

Ellen was looking forward to having her own play room, and fuck those who said she couldn't do that. Her mother had always told her, "If it feels good to you, then you should pursue it with gusto." So Ellen had. And now she was famous. Not the good kind of famous yet, but she would be. People would be writing about her for a long time.

CHAPTER 4

Joel hated being ignored. And Evie wasn't just ignoring him, but she was slamming doors in his face and just talking around him. And that butler of hers? He was acting like he wasn't there as well. And that shit wasn't working. When he shouted for her to tell him where Addison was again, a voice behind him told him to shut up.

Joel turned slowly to look at the man. He was an older gentleman, dressed in a nice suit with a bow tie. Something about him—his face, his mode of dress—tugged at a memory for Joel, but the man spoke again before he could capture what it was that had him thinking he might have known him.

"I've not had a headache in nearly fifty years, and you're giving me one. What the hell is wrong with you? Just shut up and enjoy the afterlife."

Joel turned again and saw the portrait over the fireplace. The man in the portrait looked just like this man, from the top of his head and the bow tie all the way to the brown and white shoes he had on his feet. Joel looked at him again.

"It's me. I had to stand for that picture for two hours. And I hate it. But it brings my lovely a nice smile, so I have to think it was for the best."

"What the hell are you talking about? That man is dead. I know that for a fact. Evie talked about him…what do you mean, the afterlife? Are you trying to tell me that I'm dead? There's no way…. Why are they ignoring me?" The man laughed and told him to shut up for a minute. "You can't talk to me that way. I don't know who the hell you think you are, but I'm not used to people talking to me like that."

"You're dead. Get used to it, newbie. Here in the afterlife, where you are, you have to get used to a lot of things. Some you won't mind, but there are a few that will bother you. The one thing I still have trouble with, even after all this time, is when they walk through you. Gives me the willies." The man shuddered. "Even when you know it's coming, it sort of creeps you out, as my granddaughter used to say. By the way, she's not here. Addie is hiding. From you, I guess. Smart girl. And I'm thinking that everything my Evie says about you is right. You're a moron and a bully, aren't you?"

"Where is she?" Joel decided to ignore the insult. But when the man didn't answer him, he yelled louder. "Who the hell are you? And what do you mean by all this other stuff? I…I think I'll go home."

"You can go home if you want, but you won't get any more people noticing you there than here. I can go anywhere I want so long as I return here before sunrise. Don't know why, but that's the thing. We figured it was the time of my death. Sunrise. There's this buddy of mine…well, buddy is a strange term for him, but he died so long ago that he no longer remembers what time he died, so he comes and goes as he pleases. You see him yet? Anyway,

I'll keep telling you this because sometimes it takes a while for it to sink in, but you're dead."

Joel started to sit down, but what the man said hit him. "I'm not dead. I'm as alive as you are." The man laughed, slapping his hand on his knee as he did so. "I'm a young man. I exercise and eat right. Well, most of the time. I'm simply not dead. You're mistaken."

"You're right about that one. You're as alive as me. But you're dead. Hit your head on the trolley that was over there. And no amount of exercise or eating the right way will help you with a slice of wood sticking out of your neck like that. Sorry about that. But you was gonna hit my Evie, and I couldn't let you do that. No matter, I guess…you're dead now too, and as soon as you figure that out, the better off you're going to —"

"I'm not fucking dead. And I don't know what you're talking about." But Joel looked to where the trolley had been and saw the stain on the floor. "What happened here, and where did that woman go? I'm not finished talking to her."

"She's gone on up to bed, I guess. Took a lot out of her talking to the police and all. Poor woman. I surely wish I could go there and hold her, but I can't. Stopped going to the bedroom soon after I figured out I was gone. Took me a while, but once I got it, then being with her was easier." Joel stared at the floor and tried to wrap his head around what the man was saying. As he stood there, a man came into the room with a bucket and some rags. "Oh good. Getting the stain out of the floor will make my Evie feel better. Might be a while before she comes back in this room. Poor thing."

Joel was starting to remember bits and pieces of what had happened. There had been an argument. He wasn't sure of the details of that, but he'd gotten up to hit Evie.

Women sometimes, he knew, needed a good slap. His mother had told him that for years. But Bentley had stepped in front of him. Joel tried to think if he'd hit him or something else.

"I knocked you back. You can't hit her. She did nothing wrong but be the woman that I dearly love." Joel turned to the man as more and more things started to fall into place. "Can't hurt the dead, so you know. You can...as you grow older and stay here, you'll gain more...powers, I guess you can call them. But you can't just go around hurting us. The living, some of them, can feel you, but not a lot. One guy can...there are a group of them, but they can feel you. Talk to you too, if you've a mind to converse with them. I go and see him sometimes when he makes a call out for help."

"I'm dead." The man nodded and smiled at him. He then told him his name. "Just like Mr. Simon there. Jacob Simon was his name."

"Me. That's me. First love of Evie and father of our daughter, the ingrate. But we got us that granddaughter of ours, and that's made me a happy man. Never met her, of course, but she used to come...did you say you were gonna marry her?" Joel nodded. "You're that one that made her run then?"

"I never made her run. She did that all on her own. And when I find her, she's going to pay for all the shit she put me through." Jacob laughed again. "This is all her fault. Had she done as she was told, I'd be alive and her husband right now. Not sitting here with a dead man talking about bullshit."

"You learn to love the bullshit after a while. But for you...." Jacob stood up and put out his hands. "You've overstayed your welcome. Be gone to your own home, never to return."

Joel felt like he was being sucked into a straw. Every part of his body seemed to hurt for a split second before he was standing again. He stood there for several seconds before he realized that he really was in his bedroom. His bed hadn't been made yet, and his towels from this morning were laying just where he'd left them. Joel left his room to go and find someone to tell him what the hell was going on.

They were all in the kitchen; his cook, who Joel had no idea what his name was, a little woman with an apron on and a dust rag in her hand, as well as another man with a knife in one hand and what looked like a chicken breast in the other. They were all staring at the television instead of working. Before he could tell them to get to work, he noticed what was on the screen.

"Long time resident of the area, Mr. Joel Delaney, was survived by his mother and his stepfather. His colleagues are not saying anything at this point; all of them have said they are dealing with the news at this time and may have a statement later. Of course, there is no word on the services or any arrangements as yet. The police are saying that Mrs. Simon-English is cleared of all suspicion in this tragic accident that happened today. Again, Joel Delaney, of Delaney Procurement Offices, is dead tonight at the age of thirty-seven."

"I am not thirty-seven." He was actually thirty-nine, but there was no reason for the entire world to know how close to that age he really was. "Tell them. Where the hell is Fred? He knows."

"I sure wish Mr. Fred was here. He'd know what we were to do. But getting that other job offer was good timing for him. Lucky man. But he did have to put up with a lot from that tyrant. What do you suppose happens to us now?

You think we'll still get paid?" Joel just stared at the man with the knife. He couldn't figure out what he was going on about. "I should have left when Fred did. Damn it all to hell and back. I'll never get a reference from Mr. D now."

"You work until I tell you that you aren't working for me any longer." Joel moved about the room, screaming in the ear of each of the people in the room. "Get to work. I'm not paying you to fucking sit around and do nothing."

They, like the people in the other house, ignored him. Joel moved around his house for nearly an hour before he realized that what Jacob had told him might be true. He was dead. Dead, and no one was going to talk to him. He was too young to be dead. There were things he needed to do, things he wanted to complete.

"How the hell am I supposed to make any money being dead?" He didn't even have any insurance to collect. His mom did, he supposed. She'd told him once that she'd been paying on something since he'd been a baby. "She's going to be expecting me to just hand over everything to her now I bet, too. Well, I got news for her, there is nothing for her or that bastard she married."

"My name is Howard." The man in front of him just suddenly appeared. Joel stared at him for several seconds until the man waved his hand in front of his face. "You're dead. You know that, right? I'm here to answer any questions for you. But hurry it up. I got other things to do besides babysit morons like you."

"Why do people keep calling me names? I'll have you know that I graduated at the top of my class." The man snorted at him. "I did. I have all the awards and paperwork to prove it."

"You're dead. You lie and it bites you in the ass. You did graduate at the top of your class because you blackmailed your professors to do it. And that little girl you fucked to get her to change your grades is still reeling from the consequences of that action. He's about fourteen now; you have a son. Congratulations." Howard put out his hand and when Joel reached for it, all they did was pass through each other. "Now. For lying. You'll have to stop that. I'm giving you ten extra years here on this plane."

"You mean you're taking away ten years." Howard said no, he had it right. "I don't understand. Why would adding ten years to my...death be that much of a hardship? I love it here."

"You do now. But in a few hundred years you're going to be bored. And bored ghosts get their asses zapped. You don't want to be zapped. Trust me, it's painful and sometimes you can't return from it. There's this guy on the other side...he is good, damned good, and he'll put you in a world of hurt if you fuck up. Which I have no doubt that you're going to do." Howard wandered around the room as he continued. "I'd suggest that you move out of here. In a few months they'll come in and take all your crap away and box it up and set it on the curb. There will be an auction, people will pay a whole lot less for your shit than you paid for it, and that will piss you off. When you get that way, you screw up and then things go badly for you. Trust me, move on now."

"I don't get this at all. None of this is making a bit of sense, you know? I'm told I'm dead, yet you and that other man can talk to me. You add ten years onto my life...death. Okay, what the hell am I supposed to do with myself for the next few months? I have to work." Howard just stared at him. "This realm or whatever it's called, I can just hang around here and do nothing? Why the hell would I want to do that?"

"You were murdered, right? Okay, let me give you the quick version. You were murdered, more than likely about to do something—or you have done something—that makes it so no one came to collect you. Happens more than you know. Anyway, you were murdered and now because you are a shithole, you have to be here. When you've done whatever it is you need to do to fix it, or you get your ass zapped, you can move on." Joel asked him what that might be. "I don't know. Damn it. Why is it that I have to take care of the idiots?"

When he suddenly disappeared, Joel just sat there. He knew less now than he did before, but one thing that did stick out in his mind was the selling of his things. That wasn't going to happen. Not so long as he was…well, dead. He started to laugh and then got up to look around. There had to be something he could do. Anything.

Going to the kitchen again, he found it empty, and it was dark in the large room. The clock on the microwave said it was four o'clock. Joel had no idea what time of the day that was, and looked around for something, anything to help him out. He'd been dead for one day, and he was already going stir crazy.

"It will only get worse as you go on. Time has a way of making you crazy when there is nothing to do." He turned and looked at the ghost standing there. This man was older and dressed as if he'd had a bit of money before he'd died. "I'm not here to help you in any way. Just here to give you this. It's a handbook, I guess you could say."

Joel looked at the thin, tiny book. "There's not a lot of information in that, I'm guessing. And what do you mean, I'll have nothing to do? I have plenty to do. Making money is my business, and I have a woman to find. She's going to be my wife. I've decided that this is all a bad dream and I'm going to wake up from it."

"You were killed. You were going to hurt someone, and one of our kind stepped in and knocked you out of the way. We can do that, protect what we left behind." Joel wondered if the man at the house had gotten into trouble for killing him and doubted it. Things like that never worked out for him. But the man in front of him continued. "Time is weird with the dead. A minute can seem like a lifetime. Less really when you're not doing anything productive. But when you're working, helping out, time has a way of going quickly. Your time will also be shortened should you want to leave here."

"And what if I don't want to leave here? What if I want to go on as I did before? Living my life the way I want to." The man shook his head. "I should get something for being killed. I had my whole life ahead of me."

The man nodded to the book. "It will answer questions as you put them to it. Say you want to know the date, as you've been trying to figure out, then it will tell you. If you want to travel, which you can do, it will tell you that as well. Some things it will answer, others it won't. It's like that."

"So you're here to give me a book that may or may not help me." The man nodded. "And the other, me wanting to live my life like I had before, I suppose you're going to tell me that that's not going to happen either? I'm telling you right now, I am Joel Delaney, and I make things work for me."

"There will be consequences." Joel just waved him off. "Each time you go on being the man that you were in life, you will add time here, yes, but you'll have to pay the price of that time. Do you want me to explain that?"

"No. No I don't. I don't want you to bother me again." The man nodded and faded out. Joel stared at the book and decided that whatever was in it wasn't going to be all that helpful anyway, so he ignored it. But when he went to his bedroom, the first thing he was going to do was to shower and dress for the day as if nothing had happened.

Standing in the bathroom, he stared at his reflection. The man there wasn't him. And if he was, there was some trickery going on. The large piece of wood protruding from his neck was a problem with the lighting, or someone was playing a cruel joke on him. Joel went back to the kitchen and picked up the book.

"Who is playing tricks on me? And why does it look as if I have a leg of a chair in my neck?" The book vibrated in his hand and he opened it. On the first page, a white one, a mark appeared. The green page had nothing on it, and the red page had writing on it.

You're dead. Like that was fucking helpful.

"How long have I been dead?" The vibration was slight this time, and a second mark showed up on the white page. The green one said eighteen on it. Eighteen what? But he didn't ask the book. He had a feeling he was going to be limited on the amount of questions he could ask, and he didn't want to fuck that up should he have a real need for the book. Moving through the house to his bedroom, he stood in front of his closet.

All his suits were there. Reaching out to one of them, his favorite blue one, he was scared when his hand went through it. No matter what he tried, he couldn't touch them. Not his shoes, his ties, not even his cufflinks. Joel backed out of the closet and stared around the room.

"How am I supposed to go to meetings when I can't even dress myself?" The book, forgotten in his hand, vibrated again. When he saw the third mark, he turned it to the red page. It said the same unhelpful thing.

You're dead.

"This is fucking stupid. What can I do to entertain myself?" He looking longingly at the bottle of drugs on the side of his bed and knew that having sex wasn't going to happen. The evil laugh behind him had him turning slowly.

"Hey there. You're the man I've been looking to meet up with." The hair on Joel's neck stood up, and his body felt like he'd been touched by something moving, nasty and full of things that went bump in the night. When the man took a step toward him, Joel took one back. "No need to be afraid of me. You and me, we're going to be great partners."

"In what? And if you want money, I'm afraid you're going to be shit out of luck. I can't pick up my dick, much less my wallet." The man laughed again, and Joel took another step back. "Who are you and what do you want?"

"Well, my name is Dane, Dane Glass. Never heard of me, I'm thinking. We don't exactly go in the same social settings. But I have a feeling we're going to be the best of friends around here. Oh, and if you're dead with your wallet on you, you can touch it. Same goes with the shit you have on. Watch won't work, of course; something about your body being cold I guess. And if your keys were on you, those too you could hold. You can touch them, but not unlock a door...not that you need to unlock a door or start your car. See how much help we're going to be to each other?" Joel asked him why. "Because I know where your future wife is, and you're going to help me give some payback to the bastard that murdered me."

"Addison? You know where...is she dead too?" Joel thought that if she was dead too, then all his problems were solved. He could just torment her for the rest of their days together. "Take me to her now."

"Now hold your shit there, buddy. We have to come to some agreements, you and me. Like when I help you, you're going to go over and beyond it to help me right back. Like I said, I got me a bastard to kill too, but I want him to suffer. And you're going to help me with that." Joel was liking this plan more and more. The book in his hand vibrated, and he looked inside. This time the green page was written on. "What's it say there?"

"It says that I should avoid you at all costs or pay the price." Joel looked at Dane. "Why would it tell me that when I didn't ask it any questions?"

"Because some dick that wants you to cross over gave it to you. They get some kind of brownie points when they do that. All a bunch of horse shit if you ask me. Why would someone want to leave this place when there is so much to do?" Joel told him he'd thought the same thing. "Right. Shove the thing away. Just, you know, tell it to go away. By the way, you can use that on most anyone. Just say for them to be gone and they can't bother you no more. They can't even bother you in a place where they died, either. Some kind of mojo stuff. I heard that you already had someone shut you out."

"Yeah, the man who murdered me. He was protecting what was his, I guess." Dane nodded and smiled. Joel had to look away. His mouth looked like he'd never heard of a tooth brush, much less used one. "I was murdered there too, or so they tell me. How do I go back there if he shoved me out?"

"Don't go back." Dane shrugged. "I go back to my place only 'cause I'm looking for my dead wife. My stepdaughter is there, but I got no use for her. They're both dead, and the sooner that stepboy of mine is too, I'll be a content man."

"What about my things here? I can't just leave them. Howard told me that they'd be auctioned off and I'd get nothing from it. What about my money?" Dane just laughed again. It was beginning to sound less and less scary to him, and that made him more afraid of himself than Dane now. "And I want to go to the board meeting. I have some things I need to see to."

"You do know that you're dead, right? Some people have to reminded all the time. I had it in my head that I was fine and dandy until I seen my stepdaughter. Mess she was. Anyway, just let it go, buddy. If you do, then you'll have a better time. You can't spend it, and I'm here to tell you that the thing where people say you can't take it with you is true. You can't. So fuck it and all this shit you think you have to do. You can't make a difference in the living world. So you might as well have fun being dead." It made sense, but the book in his hand vibrated again. Putting it on the bed, he left the room after Dane did. But he stopped him just before they left the house together. "You shoved it away, right? That book, you shoved it away."

"I did. And good riddance to it too." Dane looked back at him but said nothing. Joel had no idea what the look was, but he didn't care for it. He nearly went back to his room and got the book, just to keep it with him in case of an emergency, but didn't. There was fun to be had, and Dane was going to be a good teacher for now.

As soon as they exited the house, Joel could see things he'd never noticed before. Not just the colors, which seemed to be brilliant, but the people milling about. There were so many of them that he had to tread carefully.

"Are these people like us?" Dane turned and looked at him, then continued walking without speaking. "They're dead too? Like we are?"

"They're dead, but not like us. They're the ones that will drop everything to go and help others, the living, for some reason. Me? Not so much. I got me my own rules to fly by. You will too when this thing with that bastard is done."

"What is his name? Perhaps it will help me help you find him." Dane stopped and turned to look at him. "You said you knew Addison. What does this have to do with her and him?"

"They're together. The two of them. He's one of them necromancers. They try and kill us." Joel knew what the word meant, but never thought of it as being a real thing. "There are a bunch of them living up there in that house. Got them a real nice place too, but you and me, we can't go there. We have to wait until it's time."

"Time? Time for what?" Dane turned and walked away again. And no matter how many times Joel asked him, Dane refused to answer. Joel decided that for now, he'd let it go. He was going to get to Addison, and that was forefront in his mind right now. Then he was going to see about killing her, so they'd live the rest of their days together. Just as they were meant to do.

CHAPTER 5

Nick watched her sleeping. It wasn't like him to remain idle for so long, but he found it peaceful to just sit and watch her. The nurse had told him that she was doing well. He hoped so; they'd taken a great chance getting her here. When Carlton came into the room with him and Aster, Nick got up and left to stand in the hall to talk to him. Nick knew that she was in good care with Aster with her.

"I'm sorry, my son, but your stepfather is around." Nick felt like Carlton had slapped him, the information was so hard to take. "He's hooked up with another like him, and the two of them are plotting. I have heard from my sources that the two of them are looking for your dead mother and another woman. Your mother is…if you do not mind me saying, she is as bad as she was when she lived. Sad woman, she is."

"My sister? Have you heard about her?" Nick had no idea why it was suddenly so important for him to make contact with his family. His stepfather he wanted nothing to do with…nor his mother for that matter. But his sister was all he'd had in the world back then, and now she was about all he had thought about lately. "Her name is Ana Stark. Any word on her?"

"She is lost to me. I have done what I could, but I do believe that she is with someone that is keeping her...safe, I think. I do have my feelings out there." Nick corrected Carlton. "Feelers. I have my feelers out there. Should you need anything else? I have a reading lesson with Miss Kari. And her baby, she does talk to us, and it is such a joy to hear her."

"No, you go ahead. But when you find out anything, just let me know."

Carlton assured him that he would. Standing in the hall, Nick looked at the pictures that were lining the walls and wondered if any of them had this much trouble with their relatives. As he made his way into the bedroom again, Connie, Steele's grandmother, appeared. She looked in a fine temper, as Carlton would say.

"I should have known you'd have that old buzzard helping you. Should you like the information I have?" Nick smiled and told her he was just coming to find her. "Don't try to kid an old woman. I've been around a good deal longer than you, and can spot a lie when I see it. A good one, but a lie all the same."

"I'm sorry. I knew that you were helping Aster with Addie, and I thought that she might be safer with you and not Donny." She smiled at him. "He's only twelve, but I think he has the mind of a much older teenager."

"He's just testing his waters. Poor young man." Nick leaned against the wall and waited for her to tell him what she knew. "Addie is being hunted. I'm sure the buzzard told you that, but what you might want to know is who your stepfather is hooked up with. It's Joel Delaney."

"Why does that name...I think I've heard the name before, haven't I? The dead man from the other day, right?" She nodded and told him to think hard. "I haven't been able to do that for a few days now. I know I should rest, but there...Addison is here, and I'm scared out of my mind that I'll hurt her."

"It's what your stepfather wants you to think. And Delaney, he was killed in Evangeline Simon-English's home." Nick nodded, then when it hit him he stood up straight. "Yes. One and the same. And this man, this Delaney person, he's got it in his head that Addie belongs to him. No matter what the circumstances of their lives."

"And now he's hooked up with my stepfather. Christ." She only tisked at him, and Nick told her he was sorry. "They can't come here, not on this property or in the house. Steele did something to it, and now only the ones we invite will be able to come here."

"Delaney might be able to. She is his, or at least he believes so. And I'm afraid that he might be able to bring Dane here as well." He was going to talk to Steele about that. There was something there that might help them, he was sure of it. "You should also know that the Wooten woman is on the run now. The police have put out a manhunt for her, but I don't think they're having a great deal of luck finding her. I'm working on that too with Steele and his mother, Beth."

Nick never understood all the things that Steele could do, but recently, since meeting and marrying Kari, his powers had been coming out more and more. Like the protection around the house. Before any and all ghosts could come here. Now only a few could enter, and those were usually very old and related somehow to the ghosts already here. And since Beth had started to help them out with smaller things, he'd noticed that there were more and more ghosts that hung around the yard too. He looked at Connie when she cleared her throat.

"I've called in a few favors to have them keep an eye out for them, but you know that sometimes it's hard to get what you need across to some of the dead." Nick knew that as well. They had a hard time adjusting to being in a state that rendered them incapable of doing the things they used to do. "But I am working on it. It's frustrating, but I'm working on it."

"Does Steele know all this?" She told him he did. As did Kari. "I should maybe leave here, don't you think? I mean, the type of anger that my stepfather has, it might be too much for Steele to deal with. Especially with his baby on the way."

"Nonsense. You're going to stay here or I'll have to be very upset with you." She looked at the closed door to the room that Addie was in. "She's waking. And so you know, there is no knowledge that she has any powers beyond talking to you in her dreams. I'm not sure what she can do, but she's stronger than she was before. A great deal."

Nick entered the room by opening the door. He wasn't sure what she was talking about, but knew that in time he'd get it. Exhaustion was taking its toll on him. Connie had moved through the door and while he was used to it, sometimes he had to pause and remember that she was gone too. Addie was staring at him when he looked at her.

"Hello." Her nod had him going closer to the bed. "We've moved you here instead of the hospital because of some information that we got that your...that someone is looking for you." Connie told him to stop being so clinical and ask her how she was. "I'm sorry. Are you hurting? I can get you something for the pain if you—"

"You're Nicholas Stark." He nodded and watched her as she sat up on the bed. "I don't want anything for pain. Where are my things? I had...how did I get here?"

"What do you remember?" It was a question they asked of all the dead they encountered. It helped them gauge how much they knew about why they might be dead. "You were found in a barn. But other than that, what do you remember?"

She looked around the room. "I ran away. A while ago. I'll have to take off again soon if he's still looking. Which I have no doubt that he is. Are you still being bothered by the nightmares? You do know that that man isn't real, don't you? And that he only kills me to get at you. But I'm pretty sure that it's just a dream. A bad one for both of us, but a dream all the same."

"I kill you." Addie shook her head. "I see it as clear as day. I'm the one that runs you down, I'm the one that took you to that restaurant. I'm the one—" She cut him off by sticking her hand up. "I know what I see."

"Nope. You might think you do, but that's not what I see. This dream that we have? Do you know why we can remember so much of it in great detail and that we're both in it?" Nick sat down and tried to think how to answer. "And that man? What does he have to do with things? I have no idea who he is or why I'd be dreaming about him. And by the way, he's a prick of the first order."

"He's my stepfather, and he's dead." Addie nodded and looked away again. "So is Joel Delaney."

That got her attention. "No. He's a young man. I've...he's got a lot of money. People like him—bastards too, by the way, and they never die young. They linger and linger around until you want to.... Anyway, he has money to afford whatever to fix whatever is wrong with him. Physically. Not mentally, that's a done.... Not that I don't, but he's.... I'm babbling. And where is my money, anyway? I'm assuming you found it if you found me."

"It's in the safe. Steele put it in there as soon as he found it. We didn't even know it was money until one of the gh...the others told us about it." Addie only stared at him. "We've contacted your grandmother too, as you asked me to do."

"Have you talked to her, really?" Nick nodded and handed her a slip of paper with a phone number on it. "I don't know this number. Is this...have you contacted Joel and he's coming for me? That's it, isn't it? You've told him where I am and now he's coming for me. Well, I won't go. I won't marry that bastard no matter —"

Nick got up and retrieved the paper that he'd been saving for her. Before he handed it to her, he felt he should explain. "He'd gone to your grandmother's to find you, apparently. He thought she was harboring you or she knew where you were. There was an altercation. He was killed by falling backward onto a tea trolley. He died almost instantly, and his funeral is in a few days. I guess there has to be an autopsy performed first."

Addie took the paper and read it over. When she was finished, she looked up at him. He could see her fear and disbelief. Sitting down, he waited for her to talk, to say something that he could help her with. He didn't have long to wait.

"I remember what happened, I think. I was in our house. The one that you and.... There was this woman there, and she tried to kill me. You remember which one I'm talking about, right? Anyway. She was with these two men. One of them was Peter; the other, I don't know if she ever said his name or not. But I was in the barn by then." He asked her why she was there. "I was living in the house—I have been for a while—when someone pulled up in the drive about, I guess it was about a week ago. I had this cubby hole in the attic that I would hide in should anyone come by. Anyway, they came to the house, the two men, and they talked about setting up some equipment, something about catching some ghosts."

"Did they say what ghosts they were hoping to find?" She told him no, that there wasn't any ghost in the house. "But they thought there might be. Someone that they were going to capture on camera."

"Ghosts don't exist. They were just...I'm not sure. Anyway they came back in this van and I'd already gone to the barn. I was going to leave, take on another place, but I thought perhaps that maybe they'd not come back and I'd be okay. I should have known better. Nothing works out for me." Nick didn't point out that it had worked out for her, she was alive, but kept his mouth shut as she continued. "The man, I didn't know his name, he came screaming out of the house. There was blood everywhere, and I didn't want to believe it, I guess, and watched him. I suppose I thought that he'd...I have no idea what I thought. But as I watched him this woman came out of the house and cut his head off with a sword. It rolled across the yard and just lay there. I might have made a sound. She looked up at me, and I hid in the straw."

"It was a machete. She removed his head and might have done more to him if you hadn't made any noise. But we showed up, brought there on a tip. She was gone by the time we arrived." Addie didn't say anything but looked at the paper. "If I show you a picture of the woman, do you think you can tell me if it was her or not?"

"I can." Nick got up to get the file just as Steele came into the room. He introduced himself and sat down. With him were Carlton and Billy. Nick handed the picture of Ellen to Addie and wondered what Steele was up to. "This is the woman. Her hair is shorter by a lot and her...she looks less serene than she does in this picture. Like she's...I don't know, sort of manic."

"Her name is Ellen Wooten. Do you remember her? Or anything about her?" Addie told Steele that she didn't. "She's been locked up for a while now. Killed her family and the neighbors on either side of her when she was just a child. By the time she got to the Hicks, the last family that she killed, she had...I guess you could say perfected her method of murder. Her parents had been killed quickly and the others, slower and with more care. She was eight at the time."

"And they let her out." Steele nodded and that was when Nick noticed that two other people were in the room. "Why would they do that? I mean, she's nuts."

"She is. Her parents are afraid that should she not be caught soon, she'll continue murdering people. They don't want that. But they would like to know if you'll help us." Addie looked at him, then back at Steele. "You told Nick that there are no such thing as ghosts."

"There aren't. But I did noticed that you spoke of this girl's parents after just telling me that they're dead. Do you think you can try and prove to me that there are ghosts?" Steele nodded again. "I'm assuming that you think there are. That there are undead all around us at all times."

"I do and they are. Everywhere. And if I can prove it to you—that there are all kinds of ghosts—will you help us?"

Again, she looked at Nick and he sat beside her on the bed. When she reached for his hand, Nick held hers in his and tried to think why Steele was doing this so quickly after her coming here.

"I need to tell you some things first. And you should take everything I say to you as the truth. It will save your life, and more than likely Nick's. You have a ghost coming for you. Delaney and Nick's stepfather are on their way here. I'm not sure that they can get past my barrier, but if they do, they will hurt you. And without you believing us, believing that there are ghosts, there is not much we can do to help you protect yourself. You have to believe that they're here."

"How do you think you can make me believe something that no one else believes?" She looked at Nick again. "You can't think this is real, do you? That there are ghosts all around us?"

"I'm a necromancer. So is Steele. We help them, the clients we call them, when we can. The dead, they connect about their past, their loved ones, so they can move on." She pulled her hand from his and stared at Steele. "Steele here is the best there is at this. And I'm pretty sure that he's going to show you how true what we're telling you is."

Steele reached his hand out and connected his palm to that of the woman that Nick didn't know. He had a feeling she was Ellen's mother, but really wasn't sure. The man took the woman's hand, and they both sort of faded into the room. Addie just stared at them.

"This is Mrs. Elaine Wooten, mother to Ellen. I've used some tricks that I have to make it so you can't see what was done to them, but they didn't die easily. The man on her other side is John Weeks, a man that Ellen murdered at his house. Ellen also killed his children, the family dog, as well as his in-laws and wife." Addie started to shake her head. "There are others in the room with us as well. My sister, Aster, and my friend, Carlton, who has been helping us keep tabs on Delaney. As well as my grandfather. Would you like to see them as well?"

"No. Why you are...how are you doing this? Tricks and mirrors?" When she stood up, Nick reached for her, but she smacked his hands away. Addie was standing in front of Elaine when she stopped. "Where are you? In the other room? Is this a trick to make me think that...? I have no idea why someone would do this."

"You're very beautiful." Addie took a step back when Elaine put her hand out to touch her. "I died violently, so I have a few things that I can do that might help you. May I touch you?"

"You can't. Projections can't touch someone."

But Elaine put her hand on Addie's cheek, and she cried out with it. Nick knew it wasn't painful, but she could see what Elaine wanted her to. When Elaine pulled her hand away, Addie fell back. Nick only just managed to catch her when she started to fall. Christ, this wasn't going well at all.

~~~

Addie got out of the bed when she was sure that she was alone in the big room. She walked to the window seat, sat on the seat cushions, and looked out over the expansive yard. It was shadowed in darkness now, but the moon made it so she could see that the entire back yard was well maintained, and there was a large pool and pool house back there as well.

"Hello." Addie was almost afraid to turn to the voice. She just knew it was going to be Elaine and that they were still up to their tricks. Addie wasn't sure she wanted her near her again. "My name is Aster. I was here earlier. I'm Steele's sister. And before you ask, yes, I'm dead too."

"I don't believe in ghosts." She turned and looked at the lovely woman. "You're a kid. What is wrong with you people and trying to make me insane with this? Do you have any idea how cruel this is? Talking to me about dead people when I've seen...what is really going on here?"

"I died when I was seventeen. It was just an accident. Me not paying any attention to where I was going, and I fell. Steele and I are twins. I left him...well, when I died he had so much going on that day that he has only just recovered from it. Thanks to Kari, his wife." Addie asked if she was dead too. "No. She's very much alive, and having a baby too. I come to talk to her often, and the baby. But for right now, I'd like to talk to you."

"Whatever." Addie turned and didn't look at the young girl. But no matter what happened or what was happening, she wouldn't be rude and turned back to look at Aster. "I don't know how they did it, but a nightmare was put into my head and I can't think beyond that right now. Why the hell are you people doing this to me?"

"Nick has suffered so much, did you know that?" Addie started to turn back to the yard, but Aster said her name. "It's important that you know this much so that I can explain the rest. Most of it...most of what I'm about to tell you is going to be worse than the things that Elaine showed you, but I won't show it to you. Only Nick can do that."

"That girl in those...there was so much blood. And the look in her face when she did it, it was as if she was enjoying what she was doing to her mother. If that were true...." Aster told her it was. "Why?"

"Why? Why did she kill her, or why did she enjoy it? The only thing I can tell you is that when Ellen was a small child, even younger than when she killed her family, she would kill small animals. Dogs and cats, mostly kittens that she'd find and experiment on. Her mother didn't know, but her father did. He was terrified of his only child, and was ready to have her committed the week before the murders.

Ellen didn't know, of course, but when she killed them all and was caught, the courts knew that she needed help. That was why she was put away in an institution rather than in a prison." Addie leaned back on the seat and decided that she'd let this woman tell her part in all this. "You don't believe me. I can see that on your face, and that's all right. But I'd like to talk to you about Nick. Later, if you like, we can discuss Ellen and her murders."

"Nick has a stepfather. He's in my dreams that I share with Nick. How are you guys doing that?" Aster told her she didn't know. "And you wouldn't tell me if you did know."

"This will go so much faster if you would stop being snarky to me. I'm trying to help you understand. Nick was abused as a child. Not just physically, though that was more than enough, but also sexually. Nightly, from what I've gathered, and his mother knew about it. He has a sister too, Ana. She's gone as well, but she too was abused, and because of it, she took a heavy dose of heroin to end what she considered more than she could handle. It more than likely was. The abuse, all of it, was a lot for a small, weak minded child such as Ana. She's better now, safe, but she's still having troubles. Even after all this time." Addie felt her heart twist at the suffering that they had gone through. "When Nick turned fourteen, his stepfather, Dane Glass, had invited a bunch of his friends over to help celebrate Nick's birthday. Nick, of course, had no idea what was going on or he might have run then. But they beat him up and tied him to the bed. Once he was there, they took turns with him."

Addie had to think what she meant, then when she understood she felt her belly lurch in protest of the images that flew through her mind. Abuse was one thing, but to gang rape a child was something that she could not imagine.

"How could anyone do that to their child?" Aster said she didn't know. "So what happened...his mom got her ass in gear and called the police? Surely she didn't let them do that to her child?"

"Yes. She claimed it wasn't something she was aware of, that she was stoned, as she was most of the time. But she knew and let it happen. To both of her children. From what I understand, she knew it was going on but never paid any attention to it, as Glass helped her with getting all the drugs she could take. Then later, after Dane had spent a few weeks in jail for another charge, he was let out, and he fought with Nick. That was when Nick killed Dane. Even as they took the body out of the room, his mom kept blaming it on Nick." Addie looked out the window again, not to see the view but to try and dispel the one that was running through her head right now. "Nick ran that night, blood covering his body. In pain and hurting, he ran until he couldn't move. It was a couple of days before someone, another ghost like me, led them to him. Nick was dying, you see."

"Who?" But Addie had a feeling that she knew what it was that led them to him. "He said that he's a necromancer. Is that why? He was dying and that gave him the ability?"

"No. Nick could always see the dead. He helped them whenever he could. And when he couldn't, then he would ask others to help. One of the people who he had helped was the wife of a cop. A good man by all accounts. His wife led him to Nick. It's all that saved him." Addie got up and moved around the room. There wasn't much in the way of personal items in this room...a few little pictures of an older man and woman. She held one of them to Aster and asked her who they were. "He was here tonight. My grandfather. He didn't know at the time of his death that we were going to be his grandchildren, but things happened and he died before we were born. That woman with him is my mother. Not the one that raised us, but my real mother. She lives here as well."

Addie put the picture down and looked at Aster. "I don't believe this. None of it. There are no such things as ghosts. I don't know what's going on, but I'm not going to be sucked into whatever you guys are doing."

Aster stood up and her face changed. Her body, once beautiful and full of life, now looked like she'd been hit by a car, dragged for many feet before she came to rest. Her face was ravaged as well; most of one side of her head was gone. When she turned back, became the woman that she had been, she smiled at Addie.

"You believe more than you say. You saw me for what I was. Only a few necromancers of some ability can do that. I think perhaps it is because you faced death that you can. But I'm not entirely sure about that. The rest will have to come to you in bits." Aster moved toward her, and Addie backed up. "He's coming for you. He and Dane Glass. And when they arrive they will hurt Nick in ways that will make what has happened to Elaine and myself look like nothing. He is an evil man. And Joel will help him. And you will be destroyed."

"I can't help any of you." Aster nodded sadly and moved away. "I don't believe in ghosts, Aster. I can't help you because of that."

"Yet here you stand talking to me. I did nothing to make it so you could see me. When you looked at me, I was as surprised as you. You may not believe in us, Addison Evangeline West, but you know that we're here now."

CHAPTER 6

Evie looked around the room once more. She had a feeling that she'd never be back here, so she wanted to make sure that she didn't forget anything important. Closing the door to the bedroom that she'd made so many memories in, she felt as if she were closing a chapter of her life that she'd only have in her heart. Bentley was standing in the hall when she turned around.

"My lady? Are you well?" Nodding, she moved to the stairs. "Are you sure this is what you want to do? We don't even know if they'll let you stay with them should it prove to be your granddaughter."

"And we both know that it's her. But I can't stay here. Not with…I just can't." He nodded, and she knew that he understood. "I will just live close by should this person not want me in his home. But by all accounts, he's a good man with a good heart. And I've known of the Bennetts since…the son is nothing like his parents, and I think if nothing else, he will help me care for her."

"You know as well as I that the knowledge of some money to be had can change a person. We have seen it a great deal, you and I."

She knew it. Her son-in-law was a prime example of it. Bentley followed her down the stairs as he continued.

"She might have become her mother, for all you know. I doubt it. One of them was quite enough. But she might not...she might be different now after all these years."

In a way, Evie was hoping that she was different. Not like her daughter. No, that would never do. But more like her. Someone that would not let anything come between them again. Evie knew that Addie had to run. At the time there was nothing to keep her family from doing just what they wanted with Addie. Nothing would have stopped them from having their way. And it seemed that they'd picked a man to marry their daughter that was as much like them as could be.

But now, after all these years, she was going to see her again. Tears threatened again when she thought of how long it had been. How many years had passed between the day she'd called her from the bank and told her that she had to go? That call from Nick had changed everything for her. Evie felt alive again, and now she needed to see her.

Evie had put the house on the market the week after Joel's death. It was hard on her to have that hanging over her. She'd never actually seen a person die before. And when Evie had gone to see her daughter and her husband two days later, she had expected...well, she had no idea what she had expected, but nothing like she'd encountered.

"Mother? What on earth are you doing here?" Addison looked at her husband before addressing her again. "To be honest, I thought you'd died some time ago. We both did. I guess that you're doing well, then?"

"I'm not dead, no. And thank you so much for caring enough to find out." She sat on the couch that was as ugly as the rug it sat on. "I've come to tell you that I'm selling the house and moving away. Not that it will bother you overly much; we didn't see each other all that often. Why is that, Addison? I'm your mother."

"You are. But we've grown apart. I'm not unhappy with that, and would think that you're all right with it as well, Mother." Her daughter looked at her husband, Dalton, then at her again. "We heard about Joel, the poor man. Whatever did you do to him, Mother? We know that you didn't care for him, but that was no reason to murder him."

Her accusation bit into her heart like a pin, sharp and full of barbs. Addison had always been a strange child. Standoffish and a little snobbish too. But Evie had hoped that once Addie had been born her daughter would loosen up. Maybe bend that ridiculous backbone of hers and see what she had been missing. But if anything, she'd become colder, more hateful. Just like Dalton was.

"I'm going to see if I can find my granddaughter. Have you even thought of her since she left here?" Addison just huffed at her before looking at Dalton, like she needed permission to talk to her own mother.

"No, we have not. And why should we? She was nothing but a troublesome girl, and I would think that time has not changed that." Evie had looked at Dalton when he continued. "You'll not mention her name to us again. As far as we're concerned, there was never an issue born to us. When she ran out on Joel, the poor man was devastated. He nearly took his own life. I'll not have a thing like that mentioned in my home again."

"My home." They both looked at her then, and Evie could see that she had their full attention. Up until that second, she'd forgotten about the fact that she owned the home they lived in. "This is my home. You only live here because I allow it. And as for poor Joel, would it bother you to know that he was ready to harm me when he fell to his own death?"

"No doubt you did something to provoke him. You and that child are just alike. As for this being your house, I've no worries on that. You'll leave it to us soon enough, I should imagine." Evie stood then and looked at the two people that she would have done anything for should they had treated her or Addie with any act of kindness. "What are you here for, anyway? Just to tell us you're selling the house? Good riddance, I say. We never cared for it anyway, and when you die, it will be one less thing we have to worry over."

Dalton had been right when he said that he'd have one less thing to worry about. And she'd taken care of that as soon as she got back to her home after the visit. They would be notified of the sale of their house too. And if Addie wanted the house, then it would revert to her to do with as she pleased. But they would not be living in it. She was making sure of a lot of things that she'd just let slide. But no more. All her money, property, as well as anything else that Evie had would all go to Addie. Her daughter and her bastard of a husband would have nothing. Less than nothing, because the business that he owned was going to go to be hers, and she'd see it fail before they got another dime from it. Her lawyer was buying up as much of the stock as he could find. She'd have that in a few days as well.

Evie was loading her cases in the car when someone pulled up in the drive. Smiling, she walked over to Benson Harrison, her lawyer and son to her previous attorney. He kissed her cheek and then hugged her to him. He even shook Bentley's hand when offered.

"I've got controlling interest in West Iron Works for you. It was easier than I thought it would be. Seems the board is not very happy with his lack of interest in what is going on with the market." She'd heard that as well, some time back. "You now have seventy-five percent, and at your suggestion, I have twenty-four. Dalton has the last one percent. He should be notified next week when the board meets and he is no longer at the head of the table."

"Good. And you're putting in motion the rest of what I want done?" He nodded and grinned at her. "You're enjoying this as much as your father would have. He'd be so proud of you."

"I know he would be. And working with you is like having him here with me all the time. But yes, all the things you wanted to happen at the Delaney house are working through the system. There are nine employees there now, and they've cleaned out most of the stuff in the house. All his possessions are now on the auction block to be sold off, and the charity that is to receive the money is very happy with the arrangements." She asked him if there was anything in the mess he wanted. "I've taken a couple of things. Oh, and thank you very much for the new car. How did you get the bank to agree to this?"

"I have friends in high places." When he laughed, she did as well. "I found out that Joel was losing his shirt on several deals that had been...let us just say that his lawyer is not as good as you are. But everything was going to go into bankruptcy anyway, and I saved the bank from the embarrassing task of calling in someone to clean up after him. It really is too bad that he didn't live long enough to know that his firm and all his cash had been lost in a venture that his lawyer put him in."

After she told him where she was headed, he told her that there were a number of people interested in her home. Mostly big conglomerates that wanted to use the house as a retreat, but she didn't care so long as it was gone. There were a lot of good memories in the house, but they were covered up by the bad ones. She asked him about the house her daughter lived in.

"They will be notified soon after you're gone. I'm waiting, I hope you don't mind. When this house is sold and the business is taken care of the way you want, you know that I'm going to have to talk to Addie, your granddaughter. She'll have a lot of things to sign when this is done. You will tell her what she's going to be worth, won't you?" Nodding, she started for the car, trying not to think how upset Addie was going to be with her. "Evie, do you have any idea how much you're going to be giving your granddaughter when you pass? I mean, including the sale of the house and everything else."

"Yes I do, Benson. Right to the penny. Four hundred twenty-three billion, seven hundred fifty-three million, nine hundred thousand, sixty-seven dollars and five cents. As of nine this morning, anyway." He nodded and they both looked at Bentley when he swore. "Bentley, are you all right?"

"I am, my lady." He laughed a little. "I'm hoping that my name is in that will somewhere. I could use me a bit of that now and then."

Evie winked at Benson, who only nodded. Yes, her Bentley was in the will. The man would never have to work again should he not want to, and his beloved daughter and grandchildren would be taken care of for the rest of their days as well. As would their family after them. Evie took care of those she loved.

As soon as Benson left, she and Bentley got into the car. They were traveling as far as they chose to tonight, then more tomorrow and the next day. The plan was to drive willy nilly like this to keep her granddaughter safe. There were a lot of people out there that would love to get their hands on her, and Evie hoped that anyone attempting to follow her to Addie would be thwarted. Even as old as she was, she was like a little girl excited for the next adventure. When they stopped to have dinner, she smiled at Bentley.

"You do know that this will work out, don't you?" He nodded at her as he bit into his salmon. She waited until he was finished before she continued. "I'm leaving you five million dollars. And the house in Paris to use as you wish."

He nearly choked to death. She was up and out of her chair before the waiter came to their aide. It might have been funny if she wasn't so afraid that she'd killed him. When he told her for the fourth time he was all right, she sat back in her chair and waited for him to say something.

"I was joking, my lady. I never expected you to…what a thing to do." He pushed his plate back. "Tell me that you're kidding me and we'll laugh about this."

Shaking her head, she picked up her own fork. "The house will be in your name, but also your daughter's. I didn't want either of you to pay any taxes either, so I have set it up that it's paid yearly. The money is all in your name. I have put it in some accounts, investments that will make you more money so that you can leave it to whoever you wish. I've also set up a—" He cut her off. "I have to do this. Benson said that you'd need to know in the event that I die soon."

"You're not going to die soon. You're too stubborn for that. But the money will have to be given to someone else. I've no need of that from you." When he picked up his fork, she could see his hand trembling. "You can give it to one of those charities that you're forever going on about. And as for my daughter, she is doing very well thanks to you and the funds that you set up for her children."

"I've paid off the loan too." He looked at her and sat his fork down again. "I didn't know about it until recently. Had you come to me about the money, I would have gladly given it to you. I love your daughter as much as you do. You know that."

"I never meant for you to find out. Never. It was something that I had to do, and coming to you about it would have...she was afraid you'd fire me. The doctors had to have it all right up front or they'd not help her." He looked away. "Can you believe it? Not help someone like my little Caroline? And she with them babies too. What was I...? I couldn't go to you. Not then. She told me that she'd not do it if I was beholden to you. I didn't want her to be more upset than she already was. And she loves you too, Miss Evie. You're the best...she loves you too."

"You should have come to me later, when she was better." He nodded and looked down at his plate. She could tell he was crying, and her heart hurt for the big man. Caroline was his world, as were her four children.

"Cancer is a nasty business. It took my wife when she was no more than a child herself. And then it was fixing to take my child too." Bentley sobbed harshly, and she put her hand over his and squeezed. "I just couldn't lose anyone else. Not again."

"Bentley, I've made a large donation to the cancer research center. They'll lick this thing sooner or later." He nodded. "I'm leaving you that money so you don't ever have to do that again. For your daughter or your grandchildren. I want you all to be safe."

"You know that I appreciate you and love you without the money." She nodded. "You old bat, what am I gonna do with you now?"

It was the first time in all their history together that he'd called her anything but "my lady" or "Miss Evie." Evie laughed so hard that she nearly choked herself, and had to stand up or she'd fall on her face. By the time they left the lovely little restaurant, they were both still laughing and getting long looks from the staff. Evie went to bed that night with a large smile on her face, and so much joy in her heart that she could have sworn she saw her Jacob. Her first and only true love.

~~~

Addie moved slowly. She more than likely shouldn't be up yet, but the nurse told her so long as she was careful, didn't lift anything over a loaf of bread, and made sure she sat down a lot, she could get up. Just taking a shower had made her feel like she needed to return to bed, but she wanted to explore and made herself work through the exhaustion.

"Hello." The woman standing next to a large butcher block table caused her to pause. She was the tiniest thing she'd ever seen. "I'm making bread and rolls for dinner. But I have you some breakfast here should you want it."

"That's fine. There's no reason for you to stop what you're doing." But she did, pulling her hands from the soft-looking dough and wiping her hands off on a towel that hung from her apron. "I didn't know people made homemade bread anymore."

"I do when I've a problem to work through. Sit before you fall down." Addie gladly took the seat. And before she could even begin to think that she should have gotten something to drink before sitting down, there was a large glass of orange juice in front of her and an empty cup. "We've no coffee in the house. Tea that's as black as the night, and strong. Would you like a cup of it?"

"I would love a cup of tea. And some toast if you have some. I'm still feeling a little off." The woman nodded. "I'm Addison West. But everyone…well, everyone used to call me Addie. I don't know that many people any longer."

"Izzy Manchester. My husband Jake is about somewhere. He said something about going to clean out the closet. I think he's hiding from me." The food that Izzy started to pull from the refrigerator was massive. She saw two dozen eggs, three pounds of bacon, and a platter of what looked to Addie like a ham. When she turned and looked at her, Izzy smiled. "The boys are coming soon. Most of them will have eaten a little something just to hold them over, but the rest will be starved. They left here last night to help out with a problem."

"You mean ghosts." She knew that she sounded skeptical, but she was having a hard time believing this thing. Izzy nodded, and Addie started to stand to help with breakfast when another tiny little woman came in and started buzzing around the room like she was on something.

"Steele just called me. They're at the airport. You should have woke me up. Now I'm so far behind that I'll never be able to—" Izzy put her hands on the woman. "I'm nervous. I go to the doctor today."

"I can see that, Miss Kari. Why don't you have a seat with Miss Addie here and we'll get you both fed before the boys come in? And so you know, they told me that Nick is hurt. Fell or something when one of them tried to talk to him." Addie stood up and started for the door when Izzy stopped her. "There's nothing you can do for him right this minute. When he comes in, you just give him some pampering and he'll be fine."

"I'm not pampering him." Her voice was high and her face heated up with it. "I'm not going to pamper him. I'm not sure what I feel about him, but we're not in the pampering stage of…well, at anything right now."

Plates of food were placed in front of her and Kari. Addie liked her, and wondered if she was a necromancer as well. When Aster came into the room with an elderly lady, Addie tried to ignore them, but Kari introduced them to her.

"My, but you're very pretty, aren't you?" Addie blushed hotly when Connie spoke to her. "You must look like your grandmother, because you don't look a thing like your parents."

"You know them?" Connie nodded and said that she'd known them for some time. "I've not been home in a long time. I'm assuming that I'm no longer welcome in their home. I was never what you'd call a very gracious child."

Connie and Aster laughed, along with Kari. Aster put her hand on Kari's belly and told her that she was doing fine. Addie felt slightly dizzy when she realized what she was seeing. Aster didn't just put her hand on her belly, but had reached inside it. The next thing she knew, her head was between her knees and someone was shouting at her.

From the boots, she figured it was a male. From the sound of the voices, she could hear now that there were more than one, and that it was Aster and Nick arguing. When Addie tried to lift her head up, he shoved it back down, and that was when she got pissed. Putting her fingers into her mouth, she did something that she'd not done in years. She whistled like it was her job.

Lifting her head now, she looked around the room. Aster and Kari were smiling, Connie was staring at her with some sort of awed look on her face, and Izzy was covering her mouth with her towel and laughing too.

"Now. First things first, you push my head down like that again, and you'd better have a damned good reason." Her face flushed hotly again when she realized what she'd said. Nick only cocked a brow at her, but she decided to ignore him for now. "Secondly, I'd like to know when I can leave here. There are, from what I've been told, several people looking for me, and I'd very much like to avoid having them find me here. There are...you guys are not a part of this and I don't want you hurt."

"Your grandmother is on her way." She looked at the man standing there...Billy, she thought his name was. "She's a mite more like you than I would have thought. Bossy little thing too. Should have heard her arguing with that hotel—"

Everyone looked at Nick when he said Billy's name. "Just the highlights for now, okay?"

Billy nodded and smiled at her. Nick was looking at her like she was some sort of bug on a peg board. Addie gave her full attention to Billy and the others.

"She's coming. Put her house on the market and gave your parents the boot too. Only reason I know all that is 'cause I'm on the good side of Mr. Harrison, her lawyer. Well, he's not her lawyer anymore, but his son is. Good man, he was. We've been hanging out together for a while now. And he's the one that helped me clear up my will for—" Nick cleared his throat. "Dang it, man, I'm getting there. Can't a man have a little side trip on occasion? Well, she's on her way. You want more information, then you ask me, darling."

"Why is she putting her house on the market? Wait, because of Joel being killed there. I'd say that's a smart thing to do." She smiled at Billy. "You have things to tell me, no matter how many side trips you need to take, I'll listen to you. Now, tell me about why she's giving my parents their walking papers."

Steele burst out laughing and sat beside her at the big kitchen table. Another woman came in, and after she was introduced to Beth, mother of Aster and Steele, and the rest of the people in the kitchen, they were asked to move to the dining room. Steele sat on one side of her and Nick the other. She felt like she was being crowded, closed in, and turned to Steele.

"I need to leave." He didn't say anything but looked at Nick. "This is my decision, last time I looked. I'm well past the age of asking for permission for anything. Not that I did all that much anyway, but I'd like to leave here. You have my money, right?"

"I do. It's in the safe. May I ask you why you were living in an abandoned house and barn when you had all that at your disposal?" She told him she was hiding. "I see. Did you know that he's been looking for you, or had you only supposed he was?"

"He told me once that he's not a man that gives up. I just...I had some contact with people who could give me information that I might need. Not Grandmother, though I wanted to contact her, but her lawyer. He told me...my parents made no bones about disowning me, and then Joel made it clear that he was going to get me back no matter what I had been up to. He made it sound as if I'd been out whooping it up with a dozen men instead of —" The growl behind her made her turn to Nick. "You have something to

91

say to me? If so, use your words, not those animal sounds. I'm a person, not a dog."

The feeling of being lifted up quickly made her dizzy again, and when she was pressed against a wall, Nick's body keeping her there, she looked into his chocolate brown eyes and saw something she doubted anyone had ever seen before: Fear.

"He won't hurt you. I won't let him." He nodded, but still said nothing. "What do you want? Tell me, Nicholas."

"I want to kiss you." Nodding at him, she watched as he lowered his head to hers. The smallest of touches sent her heart beating wildly. "Then I want to take you to my bed and make love to you for hours. I'm not even sure that's going to be long enough to have my fill of you for the moment."

"We don't even know each other all that well. You think this is moving kind of fast?" He brushed his mouth over hers again, this time longer and harder. "Okay, just this one time you can kiss me, but we need to talk about a few things before we end up in the bed together."

"If you want." His mouth touched hers again, but only lingered there without taking. "But I have news for you…you're mine. Forever."

CHAPTER 7

She tasted not of paradise but of something more. Her body fit against his like she'd been made for him, and Nick had a feeling that she had been. When he lifted her up by cupping her firm ass in his hands, she moaned against his mouth and curled her arms around his shoulders. Nick thought for sure that he'd just gone to another place, heaven.

Rocking into her, he knew on some level that this was wrong. Not what they were doing, but where they were. He kept telling himself that he'd have to let her go soon, to either move to another part of the house or stop what they were doing. But the moment that her naked breast filled his hand, he knew that he was screwed. Leaning his head to her pert nipple, he watched her face while he suckled at the morsel.

"We're going to get caught." He rocked into her again while making his way back to her mouth. "Nicholas, we have to be careful; this isn't a good place to be doing this."

"I can't stop." Her nod had him grinning. "What if I told you that I want to take you into the dining room, run them all out, and take you right there?"

"I'd say that they'd leave us, but the bed would be so much softer." Nick lifted her body to his and started for the stairs. "Where are we going?"

"My bed."

Her mouth was everywhere. Her teeth scraped against his skin so many times that he had to stop on the stairs just to catch his breath and to take off her blouse. As it fell from his fingers, he thought of what Izzy was going to say, but suddenly didn't care. He needed Addie, right now.

He made it. Not in any kind of record time, but they were in his room. He was so glad that his bed was made and that someone had picked up his things. Laying her on the bed, her body still wrapped around his, he pulled her hips up to his as he moved them to the pillows.

"I have to taste you." Addie curled her fingers in his hair and pulled him to her mouth. Christ, he wanted her in every way that he could have her. So long as he was touching her, he was going to be a very happy man. When she let him go, he moved down her body, unwrapping her for him by pulling her soft pants off. The wound at her side had bled a little, and he paused when he saw it.

"Please don't stop now. I swear to you if you do, I'm going to hurt you." He kissed her navel and then swirled his tongue in the small indentation. When she moaned again, he sucked hard on her flesh and then looked up at her as he sat up on his knees. "Please? Nicholas, please, I need you. I think I've always needed you."

He pulled her pants off the rest of the way, lifting her legs up. Pulling his tee-shirt over his head, he dropped it alongside of her pants. When she sat up and put her hand on his ribs, he hissed through the pain. She asked him if he was all right.

"I am. I fell when one of our clients took me over. She wasn't all that happy with us trying to expel her from her former home. She was...kind of pissed at me about something I'd said to her." He didn't want to talk about the job right now. He wanted to cherish the woman in front of him. "I'm going to eat you, Addie. Is that all right?"

He nearly came when she spread her legs for him. Her body was battered and bruised, but it was also the most gorgeous thing he'd ever seen. Running his hands from her ankles to her thighs, he flared his nostrils. He could smell her. Every scent of her seemed to call to him. Sliding his fingers into her heat, he felt how wet she was and knew that he had to have it. Leaning his head to her, Nick took his first taste of utopia.

Her juices ran down his chin, his fingers were flooded with them. Christ. He thought as he drank her down that he was never going to get his fill, that having her any other way wasn't ever going to be a good as this. When she tightened her thighs around his head, he nearly stopped, but she screamed then and he could taste the difference in her immediately.

Riper, fuller tasting, she gave it all to him. Even as he felt his own cock filling, he knew that she was going to come again and when she did, he was going to fuck her. As soon as that thought entered his head, she screamed again. Her fingers curling into his hair held him to her as he sucked hard on her clit. Lifting his head from her when he could, he made his way up her body, unfastening his pants as he went. There was no way he was going to be able to slide into her without coming quickly.

"I'm so close." She nodded and wrapped her hands around him as soon as he was free. He wanted to tell her to stop, he was going to come all over her if she didn't, but her hands felt good on his body. They were hot and soft, strong and yet didn't hurt him. When his balls tightened to his body, he knew that he was going to come on her and not in her and told her so.

"Fuck me." He told her he wanted that too, and felt her pull him to her. "As soon as you're in me, I'm coming too. Christ, I've never needed anyone inside of me like I do you."

With his pants still around his hips, Nick slammed into her. She did come, screaming out his name as she dug her nails hard into his back. He bowed up over her, his cock so tightly in her sheath that he could hardly move. But it mattered little, as her body rippled around his, pulling and twisting his cock, he came with her, crying out her name even as he felt his cock and balls fill again to empty quickly. Filling her with his seed, all he could think about was that she was his. Forever, as he'd said before.

Her hands went limp off his back just as he dropped atop her. His body had never felt this good, this spent before. Rolling to his back, taking her with him, took more strength than he thought he had, but he smiled when she settled over him, his cock still buried inside of her.

They lay there for several minutes. He felt his ribs pull a few times when she moved, but he didn't say anything. It was special having her with him, and he was going to do everything in his power to keep her there. When she lifted her head and looked down at him, he could see the worry there.

"You believe in ghosts." He nodded, not sure where she was going with this. "I'm seeing them too. I know that the doctor said that I didn't die that day, so why am I seeing them now?"

"We just made love, pretty fantastically I might add, and you're questioning your ability to see ghosts?" He was kidding, but he could see that she was scared about it. "I don't know, love. It might be because you were meant to, or maybe you have been able to all along and it's just now coming out because we're so open with it."

"What if…what if Joel comes here and I don't know it? What if I can only see the ones that live here?" He didn't know what she meant by that and asked her. "I won't let him hurt any of you. I know that he has…had this thing about marrying me, but I never loved him. I didn't even like him."

"Why did you run? Why not just tell him you didn't want to marry him?" She moved off him, and he turned to his side. It was really painful, and his breath caught. When she rolled him back to his back and put her hands over him, he looked at her. "I think I might have broken a few ribs. I'm okay. I just took a hard tumble when she was pissed."

"What happened?" He tried to shy away from her question, but she asked him again and again. Nick knew that she was still nervous about what he did, and he didn't want to add to it. And he was sure that when he told her, it would.

"There was a haunting. We don't normally go to these, but we were helping out with something next door when this man comes over and asks to speak to me and Steele. Steele is in charge, you see, and somehow this guy knew it. Anyway, we go to his house and there is so much anger in the house that we can feel it. The man explained to us that his wife of ten years had passed away about four years ago and he'd gotten remarried last week. He told us that was when it started." Addie asked him what. "She wasn't happy that he replaced her. And when she was angry, she could…some dead can move things. Others can speak to the living. Not like you and I are talking, but a whisper in their ear. Maybe a small nudge in another direction. Most of the time it's harmless. Other times, like with this woman, it was violent. Hurtful to the new couple."

"She made them do things that they wouldn't normally do?" He nodded and tried to think how to tell her. "You can't just leave it at that. What sort of things? Bad? Illegal?"

"No. She wanted the new wife to hurt her son. She'd been widowed before as well, and she had a little boy. Peggy, the ghost, was trying to get the mother to harm…kill the boy." She asked him how that had gotten him hurt. "She entered me when I told her she was being a bad person and that she should be ashamed of herself."

"Entered you how?" He stared at her, just waiting for her to get it. "You mean that her ghostly body entered yours and she took you over?"

"Yes. But it really doesn't take me over. I can feel the temper, if there is one. The person's words will come from them, but I speak them. I usually have complete control should I need it, but it wasn't like that with this one. Angry ghosts are stronger than ones that simply walk around." When she got up off the bed, he had a second to marvel at her luscious body. Then she pulled his shirt over her head, and he liked that as well. Taking the sheet and covering his own body, he stayed on the bed when she went to the window seat and looked at him. "Tell me what you're thinking. I mean, whatever it is, it's not as bad as you think it might be."

"Can she…can any of them do this without your permission?" He shook his head, then nodded. "Well, that was very unhelpful. And the reason I ask is, in our shared dreams, I think that's what your father is doing."

"Stepfather…and how do you know?" She started to pace the room, and he had to put his hand over his cock. Christ, she was sexy like this. "Can you please sit down before you hurt me?"

Her look said she was confused. Nick lifted his hand from his straining cock, and she grinned at him. Nick wanted to beg her to come back to him, but she sat in the chair now and he moaned.

"We'll play in a bit. Okay, the reason I think your stepfather is taking you over is because your eyes are brown. His aren't. I'm betting that they were blue. Right?" He nodded. "So are yours when he takes you. I would bet that anyone that enters you, that's what you can see…their eyes, not yours." Nick lay there for a second before he leapt from the bed. He had to know. It was a conversation that he and Steele had had on the way home…how one would know if they were possessed. As he pulled on his jeans, he looked at Addie.

"Dress. We have to figure this out. You might have just saved us a world of hurt." He pulled a clean shirt over his head and winced at the pain. "We had no idea that she'd taken me until I fell. It was as if I was in a trance when I tried to kill her husband. Now we can figure it out. Christ, we should have…are you coming with me?"

Nodding, she stood up and pulled on her pants he'd taken off her. He wanted to have her things moved in with him, but he didn't want to do things too fast and upset her. As soon as she stood up, Nick pulled her to him and kissed her. The thought of going back to the bed and making love to her again was profound. Instead, he took her hand and led her out of the bedroom. This was great news if she was right.

And she was right. Steele was thrilled not just to have had this figured out, but he said he was glad the two of them had worked things out. Nick was so happy that they had, he took Addie back up to his room and thanked her several more times, taking her against or on any hard surface he could find. And sometimes they even made it to the bed.

~~~

Joel hated this. Not the being dead part, just not being able to make any money. He was still sitting at a table in a café when the paper he'd been reading was suddenly snatched away. Before he could yell at the woman to put it back, three other people came to stand beside him.

He still had no idea how to figure out who was dead and who wasn't. He supposed that there was a trick to it, but so far he'd not been able to pick up on it right away. Usually when Dane would start talking to them with him he'd know, but not before then. Not for the first time he thought of the book he'd left behind. It would have helped him a great deal, he was sure.

He'd also been thinking of a lot of other things. Not just his life, but the lives of the others around him. Addison for one. And then there was his mother. He wondered if she missed him, or even thought of him. Joel thought—

"Ben here says that the old broad is on the move. Got herself a For Sale sign in the front yard with a big tab thing that says sold. Told me that it was on the market for only a few hours before they came out and put the sold thing on it. She's one rich fuck, did you know that?" He told him he did. "Well, she's traveling here in Ohio. Any idea why she'd do that?"

"I don't, not really. Do you suppose she has another house somewhere? And what of her daughter? Did you find out anything about that?" Dane nodded and smiled. It was his "you're gonna love this" smile, not the one that scared him. "What is it?"

"The big shit lawyer was there when my buddy Taco was there. He said that he served them. Not sure what that meant right away, so I had me a little look-see myself. Damned if the old broad didn't own that house too. And she's kicking their asses out of the house, along with the staff." Joel knew that she owned the house, but had also thought that she'd willed it to them so that they'd have it when she died. Apparently not. "There was some major yelling going on too. Mostly it was the woman, but she calmed down some when the lawyer left. Seems that the mister thought that the old broad had gone off the deep end, and his wife thought for sure that it was all because of their daughter. I'm assuming they mean your wifey to be."

"What does Addison have to do with this?" Dane shrugged and told him he just spread the news, he didn't make it. "You think she's headed to her now? I mean, you think that the old broad is going there to be with Addison? Then all we'd have to do is find her."

Joel wasn't sure what he might do when he found Addison. He'd been thinking of having her killed. Keeping her with him for the rest of his days would have been...fun, he supposed, but he was bored now. He wondered how long making her life hell would appeal to him.

"Well, we know where they've been. I got me a bead on them with some of my friends. We can track better than the FBI when we set our mind to it." Joel had no doubt that he could. "And so's you know, the bastard lives in Ohio too. We can kill us a couple of birds with a single stone."

Joel was still sort of squeamish on the whole killing thing. He'd never been in a positon to actually do the deed before. He'd had his second wife poisoned. His first wife, of course, was still living. He hadn't had the resources to take care of her like he did the next time, but he was beginning to feel a little bad about that too. Joel had talked a big game when he was pressed, but he wasn't sure he could actually kill anyone. But he was pretty sure that Dane had not just done it while living, but even since he'd been dead. The more time he spent with the man, the more he was beginning to realize his mistake in hooking up with him.

Traveling was set up. It was easy too. They just had to think of a place that they knew very well and go there. Since Joel didn't know where they were headed, he was relying on Dane to get him there safely. And safety was something that he was very concerned with right now.

A ghost could be killed. Well, not killed, but rendered incapable of moving. There were elements, things that could be done to them that would send them to the other side. And Joel was still foggy on where that might be. It wasn't heaven, he'd been told, but someplace else. No one seemed to know where this other place was, but no one ever came back from it. That was what it meant when you were zapped. You went there.

The rules were simple, if not a little odd. If you landed in a church or a place of worship, you were stuck. And you couldn't move out of it no matter what you did, but you could move around it. Not a lot of fun in that. Even a cemetery could hold you, but if someone summoned a dead person, said their name three times, they could be brought out of it. There was also the circle. He'd tried his best to get information on that, but all he'd been able to understand was it was round and it involved salt.

And that was another rule he'd been told about. Avoid salt of any kind at all costs. Which made absolutely no sense to him whatsoever since he didn't eat. Why on earth would he need it around him anyway? But Dane had been very forceful about the no salt, and he was going to do what he said.

It took them what seemed like forever to get to their destination. Dane had gone ahead twice before Joel was able to follow. Joel didn't care for this idea of depending so much on the other man any more than he had to. To be honest, he thought him a little unstable, but he was getting him to Addison and that was all that mattered for the time being. Besides, the man had a wealth of informants, and that was proving to be extremely helpful to him too.

Like the other day when he'd been trying his best to get a new suit. It was just hanging on the rack, yes, but he loved the color and knew that the fit would be spectacular. The man...ghost, he supposed...that seemed to know the tailor industry better than his other tailor ever did, came to talk to him about it.

"You like?" Joel told him that he did. When something hit him in the head, he looked at the older man. "You can't wear it, dumbass. You're dead. You're stuck in the clothing that you died in. But there are things you can do to change up your clothing. Take off your jacket. Remove your tie. And the best part is, you no longer have to worry about it needing pressed should you leave it wadded up in your pocket. It'll be just as fresh as the day you put it on. The blood will stay, but the rest will look nice. Don't remember where you took it off? No problems there, either. It's yours, and with you all the time should you want it."

Joel had been playing with his outfit for hours now. He hated that it was always the same one, but he liked that he didn't have to look like it. Dane, he noticed, was wearing the same nasty looking shirt and pants he'd been murdered in. Even the blood on the front he sort of wore like a badge was something he took pains to show off. The man was a complete moron about a great many things so far as Joel was concerned.

He decided quickly that this area of Ohio was a dump. There was a mall nearby that he wouldn't have stepped foot in, a movie theater that boasted only six movies at all times, and a selection of restaurants that would have kept him from ever going out to eat. It wasn't up to his standards at all.

"You really are a snob, aren't you?" Joel looked at Dane. "Who gives a shit about the quality of the mall? It's not like you're going to be shopping there. And believe it or not, they don't deliver food to the dead. It's one of their rules or something. And what the fuck do you care if there ain't no movies you want to see? It's not like you're gonna have to pay when you go in. Nobody gives two fucks about you anymore."

"I care. There are things that I just like. Places I like to see. Addison should know better than to plop her ass down in a place like this. It's not even up to her standards. When she's with me, things are going to be put to rights. We'll visit places together. Make our own rules."

Dane just laughed at him. The man was getting on his last nerve, and he could not wait to get rid of him for good. Joel had been thinking about that too…ways to rid the world of this man. It wasn't like he was going to kill him, but to shove him away was becoming more and more appealing all the time.

They looked around the area for several hours. Joel realized at one point that his feet didn't hurt, nor was he tired. When he commented on it, Dane looked as if he was going to tell him he was dead again, a term he was tired of hearing, when one of the others with them spoke up.

"You don't hurt for obvious reasons. But the fact that you're not tired is something that I noticed about you too. I have to rest...which means that I have to go back to the place I died at and just hang out there. Not sure why about that, but when I leave, or when I can leave, I usually feel pretty good. But you don't seem to need that." Dane told him about Joel being shoved from the home where he had died. "Could be that. Not sure. But that book they gave you, ask it. I still after all this time refer back to mine."

"I don't have it." The man, he couldn't remember his name for the life...death of him, asked him if he'd missed his hook-up to get it. "No. Dane told me that I didn't need it and to throw it away. I left it at the house."

"Left it?" They all stared at him when Dane nearly screamed his question at him. "I told you to shove it away. Not leave it. Mother fuck, you left it? Where it can be found?"

"So?" Dane backed from him, as did the others. "What does that mean? What's going to happen now?"

"If one of them necros find it, you're fucked. And so is the rest of us. Mother cock sucker, this is bad. They'll have it all, don't you see? Not just the question part, but everything we have. News we have to be aware of. Things like a necro...them suckers are bad news, but it lets us know when they're going to be near us. To keep...I cannot believe you just left it behind."

Joel didn't understand the difference and said so. The man that had been talking to him first just shook his head. It wasn't just frustrating the way everyone thought he should know it all, but it was time consuming as well. To be asking the same question over and over until someone finally got around to asking him.

"You said you were pushed out of the place you were killed, right?" Joel nodded. "This ghost, did he just say for you to go away, or did he use his hands and say it?"

Joel tried to think. "He said that I'd overstayed my welcome. Put out his hands and said *be gone to your own home, never to return.* Yeah, that was it, he said I couldn't return."

"You're not able to go to your resting place. When he used his hands, he sort of put a hex on you. Kinda like he said, fuck you, you're not going to bother me again. You can't ever go back, even if he leaves the house to move over to the other side." Joel wished the hell there was a handbook. Then he remembered that he'd had one and left it behind, and wanted to scream out his frustrations.

"I'll just go and get the book." The man was shaking his head. "Why not? It's more than likely still there. I can just sort of pop in and pop out with it. No one will even know that I left it behind."

"You did though, didn't you? And by now, somebody has found it. Might be lucky and it's only a living human, but with the shit that has been going with you since your demise, I'd bet some necro has it about now." Joel thought the man was right. His luck hadn't been all that good since he'd died, and it wasn't getting any better. When Dane disappeared, Joel figured he was scoping out the area, but when the rest of the men left him, Joel knew he was on his own.

CHAPTER 8

Billy waited for as long as he could before he decided he was leaving. He'd been checking out the Delaney house for several days now, and there wasn't a ghosty to be found. Not even one that had been hanging around for a while. Just as he started back to the house, a woman came out and stared right at him before she started for him. Billy knew she was dead, so he waited.

"You're here for this?" She put out the book and he looked down at it. He'd seen one like this before, but it had been decades since he'd even looked at it. "Some fool left it behind. I can't read, but I know what it is. You want it?"

He took it but was careful to only touch it like she had, on the cover and not the pages. And Billy had an idea who it might belong to, but only slipped it into his pocket. His heart, if he had one beating, would have been pounding a mile a minute.

"You can't read? How do you make it work for you then?" She told him that hers talked to her. Real polite like, too. "I never heard of such a thing. Do you still have yours? I don't want it, but I'm just asking. I've not seen mine in a coon's age."

"They go back, I guess." He asked her where. "Don't know. Just back. I heard tell if you didn't use it no more it just goes back. That person that owned that one, you suppose they know they lost it? That's a right scary thing to lose, if'n you ask me."

He agreed. "I think the man in this house was only killed recently. Could be he might not care to have it." She nodded and looked at the house. "You live here?"

"I used to live on this here land. There was a cemetery here some years ago. Lots of us were there. When they put in the houses, they moved out the bodies they could find, of course, but I still like it here." He looked at the huge homes and the fancy cars in the drives. "There used to be a few kids around a dozen years or so ago. Now, all those big houses and not a child in a one of them. I'm thinking of moving on to somewhere that's a bit more friendly."

"I like where I'm at. Private like, so there's no cars and such." He longed to be there now with Steele and Kari and the rest of the men. But he'd been asked to see what he could find here to help out, and by golly, he was going to get what he could. He asked her about family.

"Didn't have any that I could speak of. I was a slave for so long that I guess we just about believed we's all family in one way or 'nother. Was a house maid until the sickness took me. Had no babies of my own that…but raised me up a bunch of them at the big house. Miss those times, I do. But things happened to us all, and I was left out there." He nodded, thinking that was the loneliest thing he'd ever heard. "I was thinking of going out to the West. Out there where it's pretty all the time. Whatcha think? It all warm like they say?"

"It's hot, I guess. Too hot for me when I was living, and I've no desire to go there now. You could come with me."

Billy had no idea why he invited her, but once he did, he knew it was the right thing to do. "Nice place. Family of mine is there. Gonna be a great granddad too, one of these days. My family, they understand the dead better than anyone I ever saw."

"I know who you are." She looked away, then at him. "You're with that Steele man. The necromancer that helps us. You're Billy Pike too, ain't you? I'm Summer. Got no last name, but that's me. Born as a slave woman, died as one."

"I'm sorry about that, Summer. And I am Billy, like you said, and they are necros. Steele is my grandson, in case you didn't know that." She nodded. "You can still come out with me if you wish. They won't bother you."

"You think he'd help me cross over? I'm done with this world and the living in it." Billy had heard that Steele and Nick could do that, but didn't know if they really could. He told her that. "I'd like to go on home, if'n he don't mind helping me. I'm old and tired of this place, like I done told you. Some of them babies I helped raise up, they're there too, I'm betting."

As they headed back to his home, Billy talked to her as if he'd known her his entire life. She might have been uneducated, but she was worldly smart and she had a good sense of humor too. By the time he was feeling his own earth under his feet, he knew as much about her as she did him. Which, in his estimations, was a lot.

He found Connie and Aster at the little cemetery talking to Mitch. He told them what had happened at the house.

"And you have this book now?" Billy nodded and held it out to Mitch. "I can't touch it. I'm not sure why I know that, but it'll cause me a world of hurt if I do. I think this calls for someone stronger than me. Like Steele or Nick. They're the only two that I know that can maybe take this."

As they made their way to the house, Billy told them what Summer wanted. Connie told her that if anyone could do it, then Steele could. Aster was very quiet.

When they entered the house, it nearly had him backing up. An argument was going full swing, and he watched in astonishment as Addie was right up in Steele's face. Kari was laughing so hard that she was holding on to Nick, and Izzy and Jake were standing out of the way. The rest of them were there too—Ray, Drew, Hugh, and Nick. Landon was sitting on the counter seemingly just taking it all in.

"I'm not one of your minions, you jackass, and you will not order me around like one." Steele started to laugh, and Billy wondered if she'd already hit him in the head. The boy had to know better than to laugh at a woman when she could hear you. "When I tell you that I feel just fine, you can either believe me or not, but keep your fucking advice to yourself."

"I just figured that since you and Nick have become…close, that you would be better off taking it easy and let the doctor check you out when he gets here. It's no problem whatsoever, and I think it's a good idea." The low growl had Billy backing up more, and he slammed his body right up against the door behind him. "What is your problem? Is it that I'm a male?"

"No, my problem is that you're you."

Kari started forward to presumably step between them, and Billy reached for her. He had no idea why he'd do that since he couldn't touch anyone, but his fingers brushed against Addie. The power blasted him back against the opposite wall, and his body felt burned.

When he was helped up, Billy got a second shock. Addie was touching him. Not only that, she was lifting him up like he didn't weigh much at all. Standing up, he stared at her and she backed off.

"I don't know what happened." Billy nodded his agreement. "I must have had some static or something. That's all it was."

"Billy?" He tore his eyes from Addie to look at Nick. "What happened? Did you do that to her, or did she?"

"She did it. I'm thinking it was more than some plain old static, too." He looked back at her. "You touched me. I mean, you really touched me."

"I'm not supposed to be able to do that, I guess." He shook his head at Addie. "I don't think I meant to hurt you. I didn't, did I?"

"No. You knocked me on my big old butt, but you didn't hurt me." He put out his hand and she backed up. "I don't think that'll happen again, but we need to be sure. Just touch your fingers to mine and see what we get."

"I don't want to." Steele started to speak and she cut him off. "I hurt him. No matter what he said, I fucking hurt him."

"Do you feel it?" Addie nodded at Nick. "I can too. Billy has a burn on his arm, I think. It's not a blister, but a burnt place. One on his belly too. I can feel it like it's my hurt."

"Yeah, but there's more. It has to do with something he has. What do you have in your pocket?" Billy was confused and started to tell her nothing when he remembered the book and handed it to her. When she reached for it, the book leapt into her hand. When she tried to shake it off, it didn't budge.

"What is that?" Steele started to touch it but didn't get the chance. He was pushed back as well. "I don't think it wants anyone to touch it but you. Nick, you try it. I don't know why, but I have a feeling that it thinks it belongs to you two."

Billy wanted to warn them away. He also thought it best to just take the book back and hide it away. There was something very strange about this particular book, and he was slightly afraid of it.

Nick put his finger on the cover. When that didn't seem to have any effect on him, he touched it with his hand. As soon as he covered it with his palm, much like Addie was from the bottom, Billy could see that it was doing something to them. Addie staggered slightly, and Steele grabbed her up just as Mitch grabbed Nick. Billy muscled his way to them to take the book. It was lying on the floor between them. Just as he reached for it, Nick stopped him.

"It belongs to Delaney. Christ, do you have any idea what that is, Steele?" Steele told him trash, but Nick shook his head. "It's an afterlife book of some kind, geared just to him. And now for some reason, I think we can use it."

"To do what?"

Billy wanted to know too and was glad that Steele asked. Billy knew what it did for him. Back in the days it had been the only thing that had kept him from doing some stupid things, but for a living person to have it? Billy was afraid.

Nick leaned over and picked the book up. When he opened it, Billy and the rest of them could see that it had the required pages, green, white, and red. But what he knew, and the rest might not, was that there was also a deep purple page, almost black. The book flipped open to this page.

~~~

Nick felt his skin crawl a little when he read the words written in white on the page. He looked at Addie, and he could see from the expression on her face that it scared her a little too. Turning to Steele and the others when he said his name, Nick looked at Billy.

"You have one of these too?" Billy nodded, then shook his head. "You had one and now it's gone. Lost?"

"No. After a while I guess when I didn't use it, it just come up missing. I never thought much about it until Summer here gave me this one. I was…I'm not sure what I thought to do with it, but turning it in came to mind. But to be honest, I'd have not a clue who to give it over to. Delaney left it behind. Maybe he lost it, but…that's a powerful tool to lose. It can cause some big damage to us on this side of a beating heart."

"He left it behind. Someone…Glass told him to. Told him to shove it away, but he only left it. The book isn't happy about that." Hugh asked Nick how he knew that. "It told us."

Nick turned the book to them, and they all stared at it then back at him. When Hugh cleared his throat and looked at the others, Nick knew whatever he said was going to be more frightening than what the entire missive said.

"There's nothing there, buddy. Just a blank page. I don't think we're supposed to be able to read it, just you and Addie." He put his hands behind his back as he moved ahead of the rest of them. "What does it say? Can you…do you suppose you can tell us, or is that going to cause you some trouble?"

He didn't know. Looking at Addie, he was pretty sure she had no idea either. When she took the book from him and sat down, he could see that her hands were trembling, and her knees were slightly wobbly looking too. His were too if he was honest with himself, and he sat on the floor at her feet.

"Joel Patrick Delaney, holder of the book, has disgraced and discarded these pages. His name has been stricken from the help that this can offer him. His heart is not true, his body is...his body is black. The new holder of this book will destroy him."

"Christ." Nick nodded and put his head down on Addie's knee as Steele paced. "Do you have any idea what it takes to destroy the dead? The amount of power that...I don't think either of you have it. I'm sorry, but I don't, and it's...sometimes it's just too much."

"I don't want this." Nick looked up at Addie when she spoke to Steele. "Here, you take it. You're the all-powerful shit around here. I didn't believe in ghosts before I came here, and I'd just as soon not have to kill one of them no matter what kind of abusive prick he was. I'm sure that in death he's not any better, but right now I just want to go and buy my house and move on with my life."

"What house?" They all looked at Mitch when he spoke. "The house with the green kitchenware? The black and white floor?"

"Yes." Addie sounded scared. "You were there. I love that house. It has a lot of character. The appliances can be changed, the floor cleaned, but I love that house. I met...I think I met Nick there in another life."

"It's haunted again. But not with the dead." Steele asked Mitch what he meant. "She's there. Ellen. I wasn't sure until today if it was her or not, but she's there. And so is Glass."

"No." Mitch nodded at Nick. "No. My stepfather would not be hooking up with her. That would just be...Christ, she's really with him?"

"I don't think she knows he's there as yet." Mitch moved to the table and, using a spoon that was laying there, he pushed the book back at Addie. "Ask it. All you have to do is have your hand over it when you need something answered. Just ask it."

"I don't want to. I don't want any part of this." Mitch told Addie it was too late for that. "Please, don't make me do this. I don't want to have to meet up with either of them again."

"They're going to continue to kill. You know that as well as I do. Once he's shown himself to her, there will be no end to their terror. The house, it has its own secrets, Addie, just as you do. But should they not be stopped, then they will hurt Nick." Nick stood up and pulled Addie into his arms as Mitch continued. "There are nine ghosts there now, not including Glass and one other man I can't recognize. Children too, though I'm not sure why they're there just yet. It seems to me that he's gathering an army. And we've seen what a bunch of ill-tempered ghosts can do when they get together."

"Yes." Nick lifted Addie's chin up and looked down at her. "They can move things, pick things up. Their anger can kill people, control them too. Once they are a group with a human to feed them, and one as evil as Ellen — she'll be able to feed an army — they will be nearly unstoppable."

"What does the house have?" When she asked, Nick told her he didn't understand. But she looked at Mitch. "You said the house had a secret. What is it? I have some too, but what does the house have to do with this?"

Everyone looked away but Mitch. They all knew what the house held. And since Nick had ever been in it, he had no idea. But when Summer stepped forward and nodded at the book, he knew that it was going to be very bad.

"I don't know about that house, but I got a secret I have to tell. There was a lot of them babies that died when the sickness came around. Some of them just up and went to sleep one night and didn't open them eyes again. Some, not many, got too weak to take the tit, and they more'n likely starved then died from the sickness that was takin so many. But there were a few of them that just...them parents just couldn't stand the fact that some of their own were darkies." Nick felt the hair on the back of his neck dance as she continued. "We was just slaves, you know. Not having any kind of life to go on with without the family that we worked for. When they told us to do something, we'd have no choice but to do it lickety-split like or be put to the tree. That whip...once it bites into your back, you never forget that pain."

"What happened?" Nick didn't want to know. He had no idea why he asked her the quiet question, but he did. And once he did, he also knew that she was going to answer him.

"There were three of them babies born to the master. One to the missus too, but he was so dark that it mattered little to the house. One of them was my sister's child, but she done already died when she birthed him. There was one that was birthed to the woman that did the baking too. She had herself a right fine boy, too. But he was light, too light to say he was another darkie's son." Nick watched her face. "Mine was a girl child. Blonde hair with these pretty little curls. Skin like cream it was so soft and white. And her little body, it just hummed with goodness and health. I'd get to see her all the time running up and down the big halls. Just like she was one of them. Then the sickness came."

No one said a word for several minutes. Summer stood near the door and looked out into the yard. Nick was sure she was going to run, not finish the story and leave them with only half of it. And he was pretty sure he'd be all right with that.

"He brunged her to me that night. Me, I was so sick that I knew I was minutes from meeting the Lord myself. But the master just brunged her into my hut and said 'Kill her.' Like she was nothing more than a hog that was to be butchered on a spit." She didn't turn around, but pulled a locket from under her dress and kissed it. "She weren't sick. Not one bit. But the others were in the house. The missus had done went over. The boys, his only ones, had already died the week before. The house was near gone. But he didn't want her no more, he told me. 'Kill her,' he said to me. And left."

Addie wiped at the tears streaming down her face. Aster left them, her body nearly doubled over with her apparent pain. Aster had always been so tender hearted when they found other ghosts, Nick was sure this was very painful for her as well. But Summer just stood there staring out the window.

"I nearly just let her go on back to the house. I was too sick to care for her anyways, and if he beat me for it, then I would be just as dead. But she sat by my bed and wiped my head with a dirty rag. Singing some tune she'd no doubt heard from the missus of the house. And all I could think of was she had to die or I would." Summer turned then and laid the necklace on the table. "I had to do it, can't you see? I gots me no choice when I'm told to do something. I have

117

to do it or face the whipping tree. So I pulled her to me and with the last of my energy, I pulled that thing around her neck until she was dead. Her little body...her little body just went all limp in my arms, and I done killed my little girl."

"Oh my God." Izzy sobbed into her towel and Jake held her. Steele and Kari were huddled in the corner, and Nick could see that Kari was crying as well. Addie had her head on his chest, her entire being racked with the power of her own sorrow at what had been done. Summer moved to the door then, and he knew as surely as he was standing there that they'd never see her again.

"There's some babies there under that there house. I seen them a few times. Not from my time when it mattered little if a stillborn or two got itself buried without a marker to show it was there, but them babies were killed all the same." Summer turned to them, and he could see all the rawness of the illness that had taken her life, as well as the pain of what she'd more than likely done. "It holds them there. Like a mother holds a child to her breast, it holds them. They can't be moving on like they should. Once they find them others there, they'll use them babies like a fire. They'll burn them up and they'll be lost forever."

Summer went out of the house, fading from the room she'd been in to nothingness on the other side. There was no trace of her walking across the yard. Nothing to show that she'd been in the kitchen with them only minutes before but for the locket. Nick looked at it, the lock long since broken, and the little girl's face that stared back at him. The hank of hair was as yellow as the sunflowers that Izzy grew in the late summer to feed the birds in the fall.

Addie picked up the book. She stared at him as she placed it in his hand as well. He felt the hum of it just like he'd put his hand on top of a speaker with a lot of bass pounding through it.

"Is there a way for us to defeat the army that is being gathered?"

The book hummed more…his fingers burned with it. When he moved his hand away, the book opened in Addie's palm. The words written on the white page were written in a red so red that it looked like fresh blood.

"Love conquers all."

CHAPTER 9

Ellen moved through her new home. There was something so…well, appealing about the place. The green appliances were sort of an eyesore, but she could live with them. They'd taught her how to cook in the home, but she'd never really enjoyed it. Not that there was any food in the place, but that was fine too. She'd figure something out. But she had several cell phones to use, and she was excited to figure them out. Perhaps she'd order a pizza, a rare treat for her while she'd been inside.

Picking out the bedroom that she was going to use, Ellen put her things in the drawers. She didn't have much, but she'd managed to steal her some nice things. A pair of pretty shoes, a coat for the winter months, and she had five shirts. And what she loved about them the most was that they didn't have the name of the home stamped on them with her last name and her room number.

The voices began almost the moment she entered the kitchen again. Ellen had always heard them, and for the most part thought they were real. Of course, the doctors at the home had told her that they weren't, so she'd just talk to them with her mind and not her mouth. It had been what they'd wanted, and to get what she wanted she did as they demanded. It had gotten her out, after all.

"I'm here, you fucking bitch, listen to me." Ellen looked in the direction of the voice and could see something, but was not at all sure what. "Just concentrate. Christ, you're as bad as that other fuck that I tried to work with."

"I'm not a fuck, and you should keep your tongue behind your teeth." She'd heard that in a movie once and had always wanted to use it. "*You* have to concentrate or I'll never be able to see you. Just think of yourself as being whole for me."

His laughter made her smile. She'd heard that sort of laughter before. Some of the others in the home, the insane ones, would laugh like that when they had something going on. Usually they'd pissed themselves or were about to come. They'd masturbate at the drop of the hat sometimes.

He faded in and out for a few seconds, but enough for her to find him to touch him. When she did, the power that came from him nearly had her climax. It was like...wow. He seemed to have felt it too.

"You're not dead and you can look at me." She nodded and moved away from him. There was just too much of him in the big kitchen, and she felt dirty at the same time, a feeling she'd never felt in her entire life. "You're not bad looking. Could use some cleaning up a bit. Who chopped off your hair?"

"I did. It was getting in my face. And they wanted too many cigarettes to cut it for me and I was trying to be good. I don't suppose you have one, do you?" He actually checked his pockets. "You're not too bright, are you?"

His anger nearly had her laugh again, but she could feel him. Not just his energy but everything about him. When he was close enough that she could touch him again, she put her hand over his cock and his on her breast. She asked him if he could use it.

"No. And don't think I want to either." He rocked into her hand and then backed away. "Why is it you can touch me and nobody else can?"

"I'm insane." She laughed then and watched his face. "I have all the paperwork to prove it too. Spent a long time in a home for the insane. And if I wasn't really careful every day, I would have been the only one there after the first day. But to get out for good, I had to show them I was no longer a threat to the world. Of course, I had me a little dirt on a certain person that really helped me, but I'm out now and that's all that I care about."

"Are you? A threat, I mean?" She told him she hoped so. "Good. I need me somebody like you. I got me a few buds and we're making some plans. I got me a bastard stepson that killed me, and I want him dead too. I figure I can have a shitload more fun with him if'n he's dead."

"Slow down there, buddy. What do I get out of this? And if I learned nothing else while locked up, it was to always look out for number one." Ellen watched his face. He really was stupid. As he worked out what she was talking about, Ellen made a list of things she was going to need. Food was a must. She could go a long time without most things, but no food would kill her. And she had to find a way to bring people out here. There was no way she could show her face around the area for a while yet, if ever.

"I got me a crew." She nodded and looked around the room. "They're like me. They have an ax to chop up, and we're going to get all that done before somebody comes and zaps our asses away."

"And this crew of yours, what do they want? Another stepson to kill? Or perhaps someone that I might have some fun with?" He looked around the room, then back at her. She wanted to get up and hit him, but knew that other than pissing him off more, he'd still be dumb. "I have to have something from them as well. What is it that they plan to give me for helping them with their little…problems?"

"Nick, he's got money I bet. That kid would have a stash all the time. Took me months to find some of them, but he had them. Him and that sister of his would hide shit from me all the time. And me giving him all that I had." Ellen would just bet he did. "And that mother of theirs was just as bad. She'd be hiding her stash too, but hers were more of the dope kind. I had that too, but I couldn't have controlled her much if she had her own, now could I?"

Ellen had no clue what he was talking about. She knew about dope, of course. Living where she had, it would be hard not to. But the rest? Why any woman would want a man like this one to control her was beyond Ellen.

"So you want this Nick person dead. And the others? Who is it that they want? And you should know, I'm going to take the names, but that doesn't mean I'm going to act on them all. I have needs too. More than you dead can give me." He nodded, the smile on his face showing her that he'd not been a very cleanly guy either. "I like to cut and see it bleed. But they have to be able to feel it, beg for their lives before I kill them. I've been without for a very long time, and I need to make up for lost time."

"Yeah, we can bring the living to you. No problem." Ellen watched as he looked around the room. She was sure the others were asking him how the hell he was going to do that. "We'll have to work on it some. I'll give you the list and you think of the payment. And we'll work on getting you paid. That's a good partnership. You and me, we're going to do a lot together."

No they weren't, but she said nothing to him. The list of names started then and she had to write quickly. There were families that were named, a few of them even named a couple of cops. As the list grew, she thought of all the things she was going to need to make this happen. First of all, how was she supposed to get rid of all these bodies once they started to pile up? A bulldozer she'd seen on television once would work out. When Dane told her that was it, she counted them.

"Twenty-four. How many are in your crew?" He told her. "Christ, that's more than three each. Seven dead men and you want me to take care of twenty-four."

"Twenty-five. Don't forget my stepson." She added his name to the list. "And once you start killing them off, we can turn them to help us. That'll make it more and more all the time. The dead don't got nothing else to do, they might well join us."

"Sounds like a plan." A stupid one, but he did have a plan. If these people had avoided being killed by the idiots with her for this long, there was little hope of her getting to kill them all. And she was looking forward to having some fun. "I need some food. Meat, potatoes. And a pizza. I want you to have one delivered to here. I'm going to give him a nice tip when he gets here."

Dane laughed again. She was sure he didn't get it, but she didn't care. Ellen was going to have fun and the sooner the better. When he started cursing, a nice string of them, she stood up and looked in the direction that he was looking. And there she saw him. Christ almighty. The dead guy was gorgeous.

~~~

Joel watched the woman stare at him like he was a lean steak. He felt…well, he wondered if he had ever felt less like a person and more like a thing in his life. He had no idea how he'd managed to get here, but all he'd done was think of Dane and there he was. And the woman standing on the front step looked like she'd been expecting him. Dane, however, didn't look happy at all.

"You just left me there. All by myself. How the hell am I supposed to figure this crap out without help?" Dane told him that was the fucking point. "You said we'd find her for me. And I'm going to help you find your son. We can part ways when we're both satisfied."

"What's her name?" Joel looked at the woman. He knew that she wasn't like him. But there was a circle around her that made him think of evil things. It was black and red with streaks of what appeared to be animals running around her. "Her name? The woman that you want found and killed."

"Her name is Addison West. She's my fiancée. She ran off and left me at the altar a few years back. I'm Joel Delaney. Who are you?" She told him and he took a step back. "Ellen Wooten, the child murderer?"

"That's me. How'd you know? I mean, none of these idiots have a clue who I am. I think they have it in their head that I'm just a wimp and they'll have to do all the work." Joel looked at the seven or so men standing with Dane. "I've been locked up for a while and I have a lot of time to make up for."

Joel nodded before speaking. "Did you really do that? All those things that the newspaper said, did you really do all that to those people?"

"I'm sure I did. What did they call me? When I was locked up, I wasn't allowed to read the papers." Ellen was excited. Someone who'd not just heard of her, but actually might know something too. "I had to act like I didn't care. You know, make them think I was over whatever it was that had led me to kill them all. It was hard at first. Then I made it a sort of game. Only three times in all those years did I slip up. Nobody ever knew, of course, that I killed those people, but they'll find them soon enough, I guess. I heard they were tearing the place down."

"Is that how you got out? You slipped through the cracks?" She shook her head. "Then how? I'm sure that…that with your reputation, they wouldn't have just let you go."

"Oh yeah?" She sat down again in the kitchen, and was thrilled beyond words that he came in the kitchen with her. "I might have had a few things hanging over the woman who typed stuff up. She had a problem and I took care of it for her. Best whole night of my life, I'll tell you that. So she had no more problems and she had to let me go. Had all the right things signed off on and out I was. What did you do to be in the predicament that you're in? Fuck another man's wife? Or did you piss off some investor that done you in?"

"I was killed by one of us. A ghost protecting his own." She nodded. "And you? What will you do first now that you're out?"

"First? Oh honey, I've already sharpened my claws, so to speak. I've killed over a dozen people already, and I've only been out for a few months." She leaned back in the chair and wondered if she had time to tell him what she'd done. It had been such a letdown when she'd told the doctor when they'd first arrested her. "I took care of the little typist when she got off work that night. It wasn't as much fun as I'd remembered with her problem. But she told me when she was in the parking lot that she was having second thoughts. That maybe I shouldn't have been freed so readily. I wasn't going back inside. Not after getting out for only one day. I'm not stupid, you know. I know that they're going to find me and kill me, but I don't really care so long as I can do that with a smile on my face and blood on my hands."

"You killed her." It wasn't a question from Joel, but she answered him anyway. "I thought you had a deal. You got out if you took care of her problem."

"I told you, I wasn't going back." Her temper got the better of her for a couple of seconds, and she took a deep breath before talking again. "Don't you want to know what I did? Everybody usually asks. But I've never been able to tell them before."

"Sure. Tell me. I'd love to hear it." Ellen wasn't sure he did, but she nodded. "Start with the murders at your house. I want to know all the details from that. They said that you were immature when you started out, but when you got to the Weeks family, you had perfected it. That was something I remember my friends saying about it. How you'd learned your craft so quickly."

"I didn't learn it all that fast. I had been practicing on the animals around the neighborhood. Cats and dogs mostly. Then I started out on bigger things that I could find. There was this homeless guy that I killed, but I don't think that should count. He was almost dead anyway." He had been when she'd gotten him to the family shed. "My dad was very unhappy with that mess."

She told him about her mom and dad. Then she moved on to her first neighbors, the Jeffersons, and finally the Weeks. That was where she'd had the most fun and where she'd been caught. Ordering a pizza had been her downfall, or she might have been out all this time.

"One of the boys, Bart, let me in. I told him that I needed to talk to his mom and he just rolled his eyes at me. He was dead before he hit the floor, his blood spraying all over the walls of the staircase. I entered the den and was surprised to see a party going on. And they'd not invited little old me." Ellen laughed then. "Mrs. Weeks just stared at me for several long seconds. It never occurred to me that she was seeing the blood of her son. But Mr. Weeks came at me, asking me if I was all right. Were my parents all right?"

"And what did you tell him?" She looked away from Joel. This was her memory, and she wanted to tell him in her own way. He told her to go on and she told him to shut up.

"The knife was still in my hand and I used it on his forehead. I never realized how much power you needed to put one of them things in a person's head before. Anyway, when he hit the floor I could see that everyone was shocked, and I moved into the room, picking up the poker as I went. Mrs. Weeks started screaming and I hit her with it. Not enough to kill her, but to shut her up."

The older woman sitting on the couch just fainted. Ellen had never actually seen anyone do that before and thought perhaps she'd killed her by all this. But as soon as she told the kids, the birthday girl and two more, as well as one of the other sons, to stand by the wall, the old woman woke up.

"Now, we're going to have some fun." The older woman started screaming, and Ellen lifted the poker and told her to shut up. "I don't like that sound. It goes through my head like a nail. Stop it."

Ellen moved around the room then and looked at all the gifts. There was a doll that she'd wanted when she'd had her party, but no one had bothered to get it for her. Her mom had said things were too expensive and that she'd have to save her money and get it on her own. But here little Lily had one, and they were poorer than her family was.

Picking up the doll and noticing that she had gotten blood on it, she handed it to Lily. When she wouldn't take it, Ellen hit her with it. When she fell to the floor, Ellen tossed the doll at her and beat her head in with the poker. The wailing started again. Just a look from her had the woman stopping.

The old man was little to no help in getting everyone tied up. She'd just about killed him quickly twice when he'd begged her to let them go. Tying everyone to their beds had been okay, but now the fun work was going to start.

"I started on the old woman. She had to go first because she was driving me insane. But she proved in the long run to be the most enjoyable. I was able to cut out her heart while it was still beating. Have you ever seen such a sight as that?"

"No." Ellen didn't look at Joel again. He looked like he was disgusted with her. Not that she really cared, but he'd asked for a story and she was going to give him one. "How long did you work on them?"

"Three days there. Two at the Jefferson's house, and not long at all at my parents' house. Do you suppose that they're around? Oh, I'd so love to talk to them now. Ask them if they ever thought of me when I was locked away. How could that have happened to me? I didn't really do that much wrong, did I?" She was kidding him. Ellen knew exactly what she'd done, and what else she was going to do too. "I killed another family as soon as I was out. They lived here too. The Hicks family. They were not as much fun as

I'd hoped. I guess I had a lot of pent up anger by then. I pretended to really like the oldest son. He was such a drip. But he led me right to his family, and who was I to turn them down?"

"What are you going to do to my fiancée when she gets here? I mean, I can't help you that much, but I'd really like to be here when you're working on her." Ellen looked at Joel and could see something in his eyes, but was not sure what it was. Anger? Sickness? She had no idea but asked him why. "Because I told her that I never give up on something once I've made up my mind. And my mind was made up to have her. She's mine. Now and forever."

Ellen got up and got her a glass of water. She could hardly contain herself over this news. It was as if they were meant to be together. When she told him that she'd let him watch her, she was happy to see him smile. Such a pretty man to be frowning all the time. But when Dane came into the room with a pizza and a delivery person, she decided that they all might have their uses, and told the man to set the box on the table. The kid was dead before he even pulled out the ticket.

The fifty-one dollars in his pockets was going to be helpful as well. But his phone was shot. The thing was dead, and as far as she could find in his car, there wasn't a charger either. But there was more food. Taking the boxes of pizzas and subs into the house, she asked Dane how he had managed it.

"We can tell some of them what to do. Like whisper in their ears to do this or that. One time I had me one of those big money trucks open up his back doors and walk away. But he didn't get far before the cops that was around when you don't need them brought him back. Nobody got a dime of that money either."

Stashing away the food, she looked at her dead pizza boy. They were no fun at all when they didn't scream. She should have been more careful. Ellen moved the body off the floor and to the basement door. She was ready to kick him down there when she saw something moving.

"What is that?" Dane moved to look over her shoulder and told her he didn't see anything. "You have more deadies down there? More like you? Go look." Dane moved down the stairs and Ellen looked for Joel. She wanted to ask his advice on how to best keep the smell out of the house, but he was gone. Dane came up a few minutes later and told her that there wasn't a thing down there. "I know I saw something. I'm going to keep an eye out for them. If you're lying to me, I won't help you."

"I'm not lying." But he looked down the steps again before speaking. "I felt something, but it wasn't the dead. Not like us. I don't want to go back down there though. Not ever."

Ellen moved to go down the stairs herself, if for no other reason than to show off. But there was something down there, if only a feeling that should she go alone to the basement, she'd not come up the same again. Closing the door, she looked at the pizza guy.

"I'm going to take him to the barn. And we'll have to…well, I'll have to do something with his car. I'm not any good at driving, but I'll have to put it in there too."

Dane told her he could help her with that and entered her body. Ellen stood there for several seconds, just marveling at the feeling of his body within hers. But she also felt sick to her stomach, and hurried out to the car. Before she even got it started and moved, she'd thrown up twice. This wasn't anything she was going to repeat either.

Nick

The car was shut up in the garage, the body was wrapped up in some tarps that she'd found, and by the time she'd made it back to the kitchen, she was a mess and covered in slimy dirt. Starving, she took out the now cold pizza and ate, plotting about all the shit she was going to do as soon as the living started coming in. Yes, sir, she was going to be the best skinner in the world.

CHAPTER 10

Addie entered the bedroom to talk to Nick. She needed to talk to him about what was going to happen. There wasn't any way she was going to be able to stand up to Joel. He was mean when he was alive, and she had a feeling he was going to be an even meaner ghost. But the sound of the shower running had her mind going in a different direction, and she started stripping down even before she opened the bathroom door.

It was a huge bathroom. The shower stall alone was big enough for several people. And the wall of clear block let in all the light from the outside, making the room and the man standing in the stall a very beautiful setting.

Nick was leaning against the wall, the water spraying down over his back, and she could see the scars then. All of them had been put on his body so long ago, but she was sure that he knew each of them. Could tell her when his stepfather had put them there, the reason he'd given for doing it, and Nick would remember the pain like it was just yesterday.

When they'd made love before, it had been so quick that she'd seen little more than his chest. But she had a feeling that very few, if any, had seen all of him. Stepping in behind him, she put her hands on his shoulders and down around his chest.

"I was thinking about you." He started to turn around, and she stopped him. "I can't stand for anyone to see me like this. Let me turn."

"No. I want to see them." He was stiff under her fingers, his body a hard mass of muscles that seemed to ripple when she ran her fingers over them. Kissing the first scar that ran along his back, she asked him what Dane had used.

"Mostly it was his belt. But he'd taken to putting things like screws or nails in the holes so that it would hurt more. Draw more blood and cause a lot more pain to me. He said that it made the slide into me sexier." He sighed heavily. "I don't tell anyone what happened to me. There's a reason for it, but I don't want to talk about it."

"All right." She ran her fingers over each one of the scars. There were three dozen or more of them, and she leaned in to kiss them when she'd finished. "Aster told me that you killed him one night. That you'd rammed something into his chest and killed him. I'm glad. He might have killed you if you hadn't."

"Addie, I don't want to talk about this." She didn't say anything this time, but continued to touch him. His body was relaxing...she could feel it become more pliable under her hands, the skin smoothing out. "You're making me as hard as a rock."

"I'm going to suck on your cock when I'm finished exploring you. We were in such a hurry before, and now I want to see you." His ass was badly scarred too. There were welts that went from one hip to the other across him, and she felt her heart ache for the child that he'd been. "Your skin tastes so good to me."

When he tried to turn this time, she let him. His cock was thick and straining from the curls at his groin. When she put her hand on his cock, wrapping her fingers around him, he leaned back against the wall and watched her. Addie knelt down and licked the crown, and then sucked him into her mouth.

"Yes." He held her to him, fucking her mouth slowly, gently. The water spraying over her head and body was turned off, and she looked up at him while he moved. Never letting him go from her mouth, she followed him to the shower seat and only let him go when he pulled her up.

"I want you." He nodded and leaned back, but he didn't let her touch him with her mouth. "Please let me taste you."

"Ride me. Come up here on my lap and let me suck your nipples while you fuck my cock. That's what I was thinking about when you came in here. How I was going to do this with you."

The dream. She knew that was what he'd been thinking about, and was why they were in the shower and not the bed. Standing up, she moved her knee to straddle him when he pulled her pussy to his mouth. She cried out when he sucked hard onto her clit. She rode his mouth like this until he pulled back.

Settling over him took some doing. There wasn't a lot of room on the bench, and it was slippery. When she finally had his cock at her entrance, Addie lowered herself over him, holding onto his shoulders. He held her to him as she let her body adjust to having him inside of her.

"You're so hot. I don't mean that you're beautiful, because you are. But hot because your pussy is hot." He rolled his hips upward and she moaned. "Don't hurry, love.

I want to watch you come like this so I can see it in your eyes when you do."

Addie stared into his eyes. There was something very soulful about it, the way that the two of them seemed to be connected on a level that no one else would ever reach. As she rode him, her body swaying back and forth over his, all she could think about was that he was going to fill her. And take her to such heights that she'd never be the same afterwards.

When he stood up, pressing her body against the wall he'd been standing at, she wrapped her legs around him and let him pound her. They were hard, deep strokes that made her feel like he was trying to come through her. When he came, crying out her name as he did, she held him to her. When he sobbed, his body wracked with his pain, she held him to her.

"He raped me and my sister nightly. First one of us, then the other. He said it was our duty to give him what he wanted because he put a roof over our head. I had pointed out once that the government had done that, not him, and he beat me. It wasn't the first time, but it was the first time he put me in the hospital." Addie didn't speak. She wasn't even sure that she could, much less what she might say to him. "My mother was so stoned or drunk that she'd just lay there on the bed beside us while he was doing these things to us, snoring her life away. Her own children were screaming out their pain, and she didn't care."

He didn't say anything for a time and when he did, she felt her entire body start to chill, then freeze. How could anyone be as cruel as this man was?

"Then it was the night of my birthday that he came to the house. I was still nursing a wound in my arm that he'd given me, but Ana and I were going to have a nice little dinner. A slice of bread each with peanut butter spread over it as frosting. Dane came in with four of his buddies from prison." Addie wanted to tell him she didn't want to hear any more, but he continued. "After they beat the shit out of me and tied me to the bed, each of them took turns fucking me. No matter how many times I screamed or how loudly, no one came to help me. Ana had to watch us. I think...at some point I just passed out. I think they raped her as well. She was never the same after that. A sadness was there up until I left her. It was after that that I decided that he was going to stop or I was going to kill him."

When he lifted his head and looked at her, Addie could see the child that he'd been. The pain and the fear that he'd had back then. The emotional scarring that still lingered on the man that he'd become. When he moved her, she stood with him, knowing that if they left his room, there would never be a telling of the rest of the story.

"He'd been in jail for something else a few weeks later. I don't remember what it was, but Ana, my sister, and I were living it up. We both knew where the stash of money was kept; even the drugs that he sold were in the house. We never bothered that part, but we did have us a grand time with pizzas being delivered and soft drinks. Neither of us had ever had a hot pie until then. Mother was gone a lot. She'd run the streets, telling everyone that her man was locked up. I'm not sure what they thought of her, but I'm sure that it wasn't good." Addie asked him what had happened next. "He came home."

It was more than that and she knew it. But she watched him as he pulled a towel off the warmer and handed it to her. When she was wrapped in it and he had one around his waist, he sat on the commode and her on the counter.

"At first it seemed that he was going to be all right with what we'd done, getting into his money. There wasn't much, but it was nearly gone when he returned to the apartment. But we should have known better. When he sat down with us and picked up the last piece, Ana asked him if he wanted something to drink. As soon as she stood up, he lashed out with his fist and hit her in the face. She hit the counter behind her and just dropped to the floor. The next fist he swung out with got me square in the head." Nick looked at her then, like he was trying to judge what she was going to say to him.

"When I came around he'd already taken Ana to the bedroom. She was tied there, her hands and feet wrapped up in tape like he always did. She was on her back this time, something that he'd never done to her before. When he saw me and grabbed for me, I kicked out at his head and knocked him back from me as he tried to get me to stand up and go with him." As he continued, Nick stood up and stared vacantly into the sink. "The table had been broken at some point. I'm not sure how or when, but there were all kinds of things laying on the floor around me that I threw at him. I kicked too, catching him in the face and head as many times as I could. But I was ready this time. You see, while he'd been locked away, I'd taken to practicing what I'd do should he come after me again. And I had hidden things all over the house that I would be able to grab up and use against him. The screwdriver fit well in my hand, and when I hit him with it in the face...I didn't stop when he was dead. I stabbed him so many times in the chest that it caved in. His heart had been punctured several times, by not just the screwdriver but his own ribs as well. I never wanted him to get up again. Then...then I ran."

"You were caught and taken to the hospital, right? They knew it was self-defense."

He nodded, then shook his head and stood there before he explained. "I could always see the dead. Not a good way to put it, but I could. When it was possible for me to do so, I'd help them out. Find things for them to pass on. Sometimes I'd even contact a family member to let them know. As I lay there dying in that box, one of them came to stay with me while someone else had one of the police come and find me. I was taken to the hospital then, but I was arrested too. For my own safety, they told me." He didn't turn yet. "I suppose it was the right thing to do, but I didn't think so back then."

"What happened then? Did you get any help? Your sister, what did they do for her?" He told her that she'd been put into the system so that their mother couldn't find her, that he was in the hospital for so long that he never could find her.

"It was too late then. She'd already killed herself. I might have too if the dead had left me alone. I wasn't able to help her. Or my mother if she had wanted it. My mind was too...too overwhelmed by then." He looked at her in the reflection of the mirror. "Mother told them that is was all my fault that Glass was dead. Which, to a point I suppose, is true. I killed him. But when they asked her about the rapes or the scars and fresh lashes on my body, she told them that I fell a lot. And that Ana and I played rough, that was all it was." His laughter was bitter. "She continued to deny his part in my nearly dying from the rape up until she died of a drug overdose, telling everyone who would listen that it was all my fault. Ana too. Then a few weeks later, she killed herself by going back to the house and taking all the drugs he'd had and using them on herself."

Addie wrapped her arms around him again. She held him, his back to her, as he stood stiffly near her. When she turned him around forcefully, he pushed her away from him, but she wasn't having it. Taking his body to hers, she told him to hold her.

"I'm not going to be able to be a good person for long. This has been the longest that I've gone without needing to have some help. I go for a while and do okay, but I have depression so bad sometimes that I want to join my sister." Addie lifted her head from his chest and looked at him. "You might be better off leaving me here. I'm damaged goods. I should never have fallen in love with you."

"I see. And I get no say in this? Because I have to tell you, you're a fucking idiot is what you are." He looked at her then, really looked at her. "You think that after hearing that story that I want to just go, leave you here? Well, of course you do. I would bet that most of your life that's what you have had happen to you. Get over it. I'm not leaving you."

"What if I hurt you?" Addie asked him why he thought he'd do that now. "Didn't you just hear me? Weren't you listening to what I said to you?"

"I heard you. And I'm so very sorry that it happened to you, more than I could ever say, but you're stronger now than you were then. And I don't mean physically. You're a better...you're not even related to him. How do you...do you think you'll turn out like him?"

"No. That's not what I meant. I meant...I meant...." She asked him what he meant. "What if I decide that I can't take this anymore and kill myself? What if I decided to take drugs and become like—?"

Addie slapped him across the face. He stared at her with his hand over the place she'd hit him. "Stop that right now. What if you do all sorts of things that you shouldn't? I do them all the time, and that doesn't mean that I'm going to kill myself over them. I might hurt me being stupid, but not because I tried to kill myself. You won't either. Do you think that I'm not going to be here for you? Be someone that you can talk to? And if you were going to be a drug addict, I'm pretty sure you would have done it before now."

"You hit me." Crossing her arms over her chest, she glared at him. "You actually just hit me. I can't believe you hit me."

"Why not? I mean, when you're going to act like a baby, then I'm going to have to treat you like one." Addie pulled his hand from his cheek. "It's not even red. Stop being a whiny puss."

Nick pulled her to him; his body was shaking, and it took her a few seconds to realize that he was laughing. When he dropped her on the bed, she bounced twice before he grabbed her ankle. But before he could do anything else, someone knocked at the door. Nick bellowed for them to go away, he was busy.

"Addie's grandmother is here. She really wants to see her." Kari giggled before continuing. "I would also like to suggest that you dress nicely before coming down. She's a very prim and proper looking kind of woman."

Addie nearly knocked Nick back to find something to put on. Her shirt was inside out and one of her socks was missing. Instead of wasting time looking for it, she left one on and one off and headed to the door. Nick grabbed her arm and held her until she looked at him.

"Marry me." Addie stared at him. "Marry me and make me the luckiest man in the world. Please. I love you."

"Yes." Giggling like a kid at Christmas, she kissed him on the mouth and opened the door. "Hurry. I want you to meet my best friend and ally. You'll love her."

~~~

Evie was sort of nervous. It had taken them a little longer to get here than she'd thought, but that was because she'd been so nervous that she'd had Bentley take a few side trips and had delayed them on purpose. They knew that they weren't being followed, but there was no point in taking chances this late in the game. She loved her granddaughter more than anything, but it had been a long time since she'd seen her too. But the moment she came into the room, Evie burst into tears and knew that she was just being silly.

"Oh, Grandma." Addie ran to her, wrapping her up in her arms until Evie could hardly breathe. But it was fine...she was fine, and she sobbed right along with her. Her little Addie was with her now.

Neither of them finished a sentence. She told her that she loved...and Addie told her that she missed.... Each of them knew what the other meant, but to others she was sure it was gibberish.

Bentley was hugged too, his big body bent double to hold Addie to him, and the tears fell from his eyes. He handed her the tin of scones that he'd made for her. Told her that she was gorgeous and held her again like she was his own child come home. In a way Evie supposed she was. Addie had been the world to them both since she'd been born.

When a young man cleared his throat, she realized that the others, Steele and his lovely wife, had left them. Addie waved the man over, and Evie knew that her granddaughter had found love, true love, at last.

"This is Nicholas Stark. He just asked me to marry him, and I said yes." Bentley shook his hand to congratulate him, but Evie wanted a closer look at the man who would love her Addie. "Grandmother, he's so wonderful. You'll love him."

"Young man." He nodded at her and smiled. "Do you have any idea what my granddaughter is worth? What she will be bringing to this marriage?"

"No. And frankly, I think you asking me borders on being rude. And before you ask or investigate me, you should know that not everything you find will be right. Yes, I'm a son of a drug addict. My sister killed herself the same way when she was just shy of her ninth birthday. I killed my stepfather with a screwdriver for...well, let's just say that he wasn't a good man. But all that matters nothing to Addie, and that's all that matters. I will be polite to you, might even like you, but for her money or yours? I could care less. I have a good job. I make good money, and I have invested well. I love her and will care for her in the best possible way." Evie liked him. When he winked at her, she thought perhaps she might even love this man after a time. "But most importantly, Mrs. Simon-English, she is my world, and the rest of it can go to hell for all that I care."

"You're a very candid young man, aren't you?" He nodded and kissed her on the back of her hand. "I think we're going to get along just fine, you and me."

"Good. Now, I've just talked to Steele, and he and I are under the agreement that rather than just run around a bush that will get us in the same position as we might have should we just jump right in, I want to tell you what I do for a living." She nodded, not sure at all that she wanted to hear this. Looking at Addie wasn't that assuring either, but Evie sat when he asked her to. "My friend and the owner of this house is going to sit with us too. As are the others that live here. Mrs. Simon-English, some of this is going to be very hard to swallow, but I want you to have an open mind."

"Something has happened." Nicholas nodded. "All right. And call me Evie. And this is my best friend, Bentley. Where I go, he goes."

"Good to know." Nicholas turned and looked at Bentley, extending his hand in friendship. "Mr. Bentley."

As the other men filed into the room, Evie watched them. Steele she had met with his wife, but the others were just as comfortable with each other as Steele had been with her. Evie knew people born to money, and Steele had been. He wore it well, and she had a feeling that he would tell you that it meant nothing to him. And for once in her life, she would believe him.

Nick, as he asked her to call him, introduced the others in the room. "You've met Steele Bennett and his wife Kari. This is Drew Mullins...he's the dark and quiet kind of guy. Hugh McGuire is to his right. Hugh is...he can say more with one word than most can say with a book. Ray Hancock is former FBI and sort of the head master of us. He keeps us in line and is our savior for the most part. Landon Logan is...Landon is Landon. He's one of the most honest and hard men I know." Landon tipped an imaginary hat and smiled at her. "Mitch Riley is a thinker. His mind rarely rests, and if you stay here, which I'm to understand that you've been asked to do, you will see him roaming the halls in the middle of the night more often than not. Izzy and her husband Jake run the kitchen and the rooms. There is a staff here that takes care of us better than we deserve."

Each of the men welcomed them. Evie knew there was more. There had to be. And as she waited for it, she saw the men shuffle their feet and squirm on the couch. For some reason that made her more nervous than she was before.

"Well? Spill it. I'm an old woman, but I'm not a stupid one. Tell me." He looked to her right and she did as well. There was nothing there. "Young man, don't piss me off before we begin."

"Jacob Simon is there with you. He's been there since you came into the room, feeling the emotion that you are feeling for having Addie back with you." Evie sat back in the chair as Nick continued. "Billy Pike is here too. He died some years ago and helps us on our job a great deal. There is also Donny and Carlton. Donny died about twenty years ago—drive by shooting—and Carlton won't tell us what he was killed by. I'm thinking he was having a tryst with a married woman and got caught."

Evie looked at Addie, then at Nick. "I don't think you're trying to be funny, are you? You can really see him. All of them."

"Yes, ma'am. I can see them all. Jacob wants you to know that Joel would never have touched you. He said that killing him for you was his greatest pleasure. He said that he loves you just as much today as he did when he first saw you coming out of the Grand Theater with that fop of a man you were supposed to marry." Nick smiled. "Jacob said to tell you that the violets that he gave you still do not compare to the beauty of your eyes or the softness of your skin."

She put her hand over her mouth to stop the sob that wanted to spill out. He really was here. Her one and only truest love was here. Evie asked Nick if she could speak to him and turned to her right to look for him.

"I love you. I have never loved anyone like I did you." She felt his touch then, much like she had in the hotel the other night but had refused to believe it. Without turning to the others in the room, she spoke again. "You do this? You find ghosts and help them connect with their loved ones?"

"Something like that." She turned to Steele and he smiled at her. "We're here to help who wants us to in things that we can. We also assist the police or anyone that needs us, living or dead."

"And Joel, he's...are you going to tell me there is a problem with him?" Addie told her that he wanted her dead. "That's not going to happen. He couldn't have you when he was alive, and I'm certainly not going to let him touch you while he's dead. Tell me what you need for me to do."

"Tell us everything you can about the bastard." Evie nodded and looked at Bentley, who left the room to return a few minutes later with two boxes. There were more and he went to get those as well.

"Everything you ever wanted to know about Joel Delaney. And there are also several boxes on Addie's parents. I only ask that you let me help." Nick said she was going to. "Good. Let's get this going, shall we?"

Evie wasn't sure what to believe or disbelieve, but her granddaughter was alive and happy, and that alone could make her believe just about anything.

CHAPTER 11

Joel moved through the yard. He wasn't entirely sure why he was there, but when he'd thought of Addison this was where he'd ended up. The small cemetery had been so close to where he'd landed that he'd been terrified that he'd end up there forever. But the names on the pretty stones hadn't said his name or that of Addison, and he did rest a bit better. A voice behind him made him turn, and he watched as the big man approached. For some reason, Joel wasn't afraid but somewhat relieved.

"You're that man. The one that's been bothering Addie. You go on and get out of here. If you don't, then I'm going to get Steele and he'll make sure you never move around again." Joel was sure that this man, this Steele person, was the one he'd been warned about. "Get yourself—"

"Don't say it, please. I'm begging you to let me tell you something first." The man put his hands down, but Joel wasn't convinced that he wouldn't finish what he'd started and zap him. "I'm here to tell Addison that...well among other things, that I'm sorry."

"Why?" It was a good question. And one he'd been bouncing around in his head since leaving the house across the way. "You tell me or so help me...."

"I've been trying to find her. That's true. I want her…wanted her as dead as me so that I could rule her. But I've seen some things…heard things that have made me realize that I'm not at all a very nice person." The man told him to go on, he'd not argue with him. Joel laughed. "There was a time when I would have had you fired if you worked for me for that kind of talk. And if you were just a person I knew, then I'd just ruin you. Financially as well as any other way I could. But I've been wandering around here for the last few days just…is she all right? I mean, Addison, is she all right?"

"In love." Joel felt his heart twist and his temper flare up, but he only nodded. It was no more than he deserved. "You said you wanted to say you were sorry. What for?"

"I don't know how much time I have. I'm not at all good at this death stuff. But there is a woman…. Actually, there is a man and woman…Ellen Wooten, have you heard of her?" The man said he had. "She's going to kill Addison for me. Well, not for me, but she thinks she can lure her there and…I don't want her to die. Not like…not anymore. There's a man too, Dane Glass. He has a stepson that he wants dead so he can make him suffer as he did. I did some research and I know who he is now too. But Glass, he told me that they knew each other, Addison and this stepson."

"Did he tell you the boy's name?" Joel told him Nick Stark. "I'm thinking you should come on up to the house then. But I'm telling you right now, should you try something stupid, I'm going to send you over. And from what I know about you, it won't be anywhere pleasant you want to be."

Joel followed the man. "I didn't hear your name. Or even if you told me. I'm so…did you know that all you have to do is think of someone and you could be near them? Not Addison however. She's sort of off limits to me."

"Billy Pike, and that would be about right. This boy Glass is looking for? He tell you what he wanted with him? Other than to have him dead?" Joel told him that the stepson had killed Glass.

"But the more time I spend with him, the more I think he was justified in it." Billy said that he was. "Is Addison here? I know that her grandmother has sold out and moved on. I'm assuming that she's coming for her granddaughter. They were very close and I missed out on that too."

There were a great many things he'd missed out on. And hearing Ellen talk about her murder spree had made him realize that there were a great many evil people out there. He didn't want to be one of them. Not any longer. Joel realized that Billy was talking and he'd missed some of it. When he asked him to repeat it, Billy turned to look at him.

"You've made yourself a huge turnaround since you were killed. What the hell happened to you? And if you tell me you found religion, I'm not going to believe you. There is no way that much can happen to you in two weeks." Joel asked him why two weeks. "You've been dead that long. Didn't you know?"

"No. It seems…there are times when I still have to remind myself that I'm actually dead. I went to my graveside. Not a single flower marred the grass there. No prints—auras, I guess they're called—showed that a single person, other than a couple of men, came to see me off. As you have probably already guessed, I'm not a well-liked person." Billy didn't agree or disagree with him, for which he was grateful. "Ellen…she opened my eyes to what I was going to do. What I wanted to do. She killed those people, all of them, because it was fun to her. How could she...? She just wanted to practice her cutting and did it. Why? Then when she told me how she got out and what she's done since then, I left them. I decided that I wanted no part of them."

They were at the house and Joel didn't even try to go inside. There was something like a glow around the house, and he knew that trying to cross that line he'd be hurt...or worse. Billy had no problems and entered the orb around it as if it were nothing. A man came out moments later and Joel had an insane need to go to his knees in front of him. He knew as surely as he was standing there that this was the famed Steele Bennett.

"Billy said that you want to talk to Addie." Joel nodded and didn't look at the man's face. "He said that you were with Wooten and Glass, and now have had a change of heart on a few things."

"They're gathering an army." It sounded so stupid when he said it aloud that he looked at the man. "You're him, aren't you? Steele. I've heard so much about you that I'm sort of thinking I'm going to wet myself, but I know that's not possible."

"No, it's not. But you fuck up here, and I will make sure you're never seen again. I'm Steele and you're Joel Delaney. I heard that you were looking to bring Addie to your side. You know that it doesn't work that way, right?" Joel told him he had no idea how any of this worked. "Yeah, you left your book behind."

Joel looked at him then. The man was bathed in light, bright white light that hurt his eyes. If he had his book, then all was lost for him. But it mattered very little right now. He had to tell them what he knew.

"Ellen is going to bring the living to her. She has a bunch of cell phones and some money now. Glass and his men, six of them when I was there, are whispering in the ears of the living and having them go out to this house in the middle of nowhere." Steele was joined by a woman and she glowed as well. Joel continued, but he knew that he was somewhat babbling and tried to calm his thoughts. "Ellen has a house that she's using as a base, I guess you could call it. She's planning to fill the yard with the dead after she's finished with them. While I was there a...I don't want you to think I had anything to do with it, but when I was there, she cut the throat of a pizza delivery person. Perfect her art, is what she called it. Get perfect at it until she can have Addison and this other man, Nick Stark, brought to her and make them suffer for us. I never wanted her to suffer. And to be honest, I'm not sure why I even...it matters little now. But I want—"

"I want to know." He looked at the doorway and nearly sobbed in relief. There she was, Addison in the flesh. "Even after five years of me being gone, why did you keep sending people to find me? What did you hope to gain by that? I never wanted to marry you, but you were...you just didn't let it go. Why?"

"I don't know. You were mine and that's all I could see." He looked at the man who stood next to her. "You're in love with him. I can see it. You're glowing with it. Christ, that could have been mine had I been a good deal smarter."

"I was never meant for you, Joel. You know that, don't you?" He nodded at her. "Billy said that you wanted to help us. He said that you have information on where Glass is."

"There's a woman after you and this man, Glass, is after a man by the name of Nick. I was wondering if you could get him some...." Joel looked at them all when they laughed. "I don't understand. He can hurt him."

Steele stood up and Joel took a step back. "Joel Delaney, I want you to meet Addie's fiancé, Nick Stark. Nick, this is the man that is going to help us bring Ellen Wooten to an end."

~~~

Nick tried to be nice to the man. Steele hadn't allowed him into the house as yet, and while Joel didn't seem to have a problem with it, Nick knew that the guy was still out there. He walked to the window and looked out to the cemetery at the back of the property.

"You do know that there is nothing out there that can hurt either of us, right? I mean, we can fight this thing, and Steele has sent some of the others out to the house to keep an eye on them. I had no idea the guy was so strong." Nick didn't even turn to look at Addie when she spoke to him, but answered her as he watched the yard.

"Steele is the strongest necromancer I've ever met. More than likely the strongest ever born. He can do more things with his power than most people can do...well, anything." He turned then and saw her sitting on the edge of the bed. "You're so beautiful."

"Thank you. You're very handsome." She crooked her finger at him. "Come here, Nick. I have a powerful need to have you inside of me."

Nick didn't move to her but leaned back against the wall and watched her. He wanted her. Wanting her with every breath, he took every minute of the day and then some. But he also knew that in a moment, less than a heartbeat, he could lose her. And that terrified him more than anything.

"Stand up and take off your clothes. I want you to undress for me." Instead of doing what he wanted, she leaned back on the bed. Nick started to ask her again when she kicked off her shoes. Then she sat up and pulled her socks off.

Nick loved a woman's legs. The way that the muscles seemed curve into an incredibly sexy form, the way they hardened at just the right moment when the foot was lifted from the floor. He thought that high heels should be worn at all times by them, and that pantyhose should be outlawed and those stocking that were held up by gravity should be the norm. But watching Addie pull off a simple pair of athletic socks nearly had him moaning.

When she stood up, he nearly left his post. But if he was honest with himself, he was afraid he'd fall on his face before he got more than a foot from it. He was that enthralled by her sheer beauty.

The buttons on her blouse were undone slowly. He watched as she moved her fingers slowly over a tiny little button and then worked it through the equally small hole. As she moved her fingers down to the next one, he had to cup his cock. He'd seen nothing but her feet since he'd asked her to do this, and he could see that he more than likely wasn't going to make it until she was completely undressed.

The blouse was unbuttoned but stayed on her body. He had no idea why that was as sexy as hell, but he loved it. As she moved her hand down her belly to the top of her pants, he licked his suddenly dry lips and watched. The sound of the button coming undone nearly had him dropping to his knees and begging her for more.

"You're very hard, aren't you?" He nodded, no longer able to think beyond what she was doing. "I want to see you, Nicholas. Take out your lovely cock and let me see you."

"If I do, then I'm going to come. The slightest breath of air over me is going to be my undoing." Her soft laughter had him reaching for his belt. When he pulled it open, his cock seemed to stretch more, fill his pants to a painful degree. "I love what you're doing right now. Christ, I want to jump on you and take you hard."

"No. Not yet." He nodded, feeling like a simpleton. "When I'm naked, and I will be soon, I'm going to lie back on this bed and play with myself while you watch. Then when I say so, you can come here and eat me until I come."

"Hurry." She laughed again, and Nick felt like he was going to die. It was going to be a wonderfully fulfilling death, seeing her like this, but he was a dead man all the same. "I need you."

"As I do you." The pants were open, her panties there for him to see. The bit of lace—pink, he thought—was going to be twice as beautiful laying on the floor. But not soon enough so far as his body was concerned. "Did you know that Kari was a panther?"

Nick's fuzzed mind had no idea what she was saying to him, and he asked her to repeat it. Or at least that was what he'd meant. What spilled from his mouth was gibberish, and she laughed again.

"Kari? Yes. Panther. She was converted by a madman." Addie moved her hands into the front of her jeans and he heard her moan. "She's beautiful as a panther. Are you wet?"

"I'm very wet." He knew that her fingers were sliding over her pussy, touching her clit and making the little nubbin harder. "I saw her. As a panther this morning. She scared me. I'm so close to coming, Nicholas. I might not be able to wait for you."

He'd had enough. Taking the final steps to her, he dropped to his knees and jerked her pants off. Nick was right, her fingers were deep in her panties and she was soaking wet. Burying his nose into the wet silk, he inhaled deeply, taking all of her scent into his body.

"Come." She screamed out his name as her fingers danced beneath the cloth. He could smell her, the delicious smell that was all her. Tearing her panties from her, he licked her fingers clean, then told her to lie back on the bed. Nick was going to enjoy this.

Nick spread her legs wide. Her clit was so swollen that it peeked out from her swollen nether lips, and he leaned in to taste it. But taking the tiny pearl into his mouth, he couldn't help but slide his fingers into her sheath to bring her again. When she came this time, Nick felt her juices run down his hand to his elbow as he tried to drink every drop of her.

As she rode his mouth, he freed his cock. He was painfully hard, and when he fisted himself, he moaned against her pussy and nearly came. Christ, he'd never been this hard in his life, and he pulled away from her to move up her body.

Standing up, he watched her slide to the middle of the bed. Nick held his cock and cupped his balls while he waited for her. It was that or hurt more. When she opened her thighs and put her hands over her hard nipples, Nick couldn't wait any longer. Letting himself go, he moved up the bed. But he had a few bites of paradise on the way up.

Her hip tasted of dew. Her navel reminded him of deep waters in the oceans, mystical and beautiful. When he licked her nipple, then took the tip into his mouth, all he could think about was suckling until he came on her, but her hips came up and her heat scorched his cock. Holding his cock while he continued to suckle at her breast, Nick entered her slowly.

Nick buried himself to his root and stilled. It was that or come right then. When she wrapped her feet over his calves and moved upward, taking him deeper still, he kissed her, moving his tongue within the dark sweetness that was her. He finally moved, slowly at first and then more as she rolled her hips up to meet him.

Cupping her ass, Nick brought her to him. Hard strokes...he had to have her, had to come deep within her, and right now. When she dug her nails into his shoulder, he felt her tear into his skin and knew that she'd drawn blood. When he felt her tighten around him, her body bow upward and every part of her tense, Nick watched her face as she came again, screaming out her release that had him marvel again at her beauty. When she screamed again, telling him that she was coming again, Nick let himself take his own pleasure, pounding hard into her until his cock simply exploded his release deep within her.

As she came a third time, her hands pulling him to her, Nick kissed her again, fucking her mouth with hard sure strokes like his cock was doing to her pussy. When his balls tightened again, heralding another powerful climax, Nick threw back his head and roared. He felt his release all the way from his toes to the top of his head as he emptied himself inside of her again.

Her slight giggle had him using what tiny little bit of strength he had to lift his head. Nick wouldn't have believed it possible, but he was sure that she was more beautiful now than she'd ever been, and he fell in love with her again. Kissing her on the nose, he rolled them to his back and held her.

"What was all that about Kari?" He knew that Addie had nearly been asleep, but it just occurred to him what she'd said earlier. "You had to bring her up just then?"

"I was trying to think of a way to slow me down. All I wanted to do was just come right then, and I wanted to tease you more." She lifted her head from his chest and frowned. "She really is a panther. I mean, I saw her and everything, but she scared the shit out of me."

"I should have told you. Or one of us should have. She really was changed against her will, and Steele has found her a teacher to guide her through some of the things she wasn't trained on." Nick thought of the pretty little panther that he'd seen a week ago and wondered if Steele had had any luck bringing the little cub to the house. "When you walk the grounds, be careful of the cub, the little panther that is roaming the grounds. I don't know if she's wild or not, but she's a little thing and scared to death. I meant to ask someone how to tell, but it wouldn't matter since she runs when I get close to her."

"I was watching her when Kari came up behind me. I thought for sure she was her mother, but Kari told me that she'd been tracking her for days and that was the first time she'd been close enough to her. She's a panther, not a shifter. Kari told me." Addie laid her head back down on his chest. "Steele told me that you guys are going to the house tomorrow to confront Ellen. I would like to go."

Nick wanted her there too, if for no other reason than he wanted her close to him. But she had little to no experience dealing with the dead, much less a living monster, and thought it was a good idea that she and Kari stayed here. He told her that and she nodded.

"Do you want to live here for a while, or did you want to find us a place close to here? I know that your grandmother has decided to buy. She even told me that she'd like for us to live with her and Bentley until we get us a house." Addie sat up over him again. "I don't care where we live so long as I'm with you."

"I've missed her." He nodded. He wasn't close to his own family and never would be, but he could see the love that the three of them, Bentley included, had for each other. "I know that this house is huge and all, but I'd really like our own home. With Grandmother."

"Then we'll tell her." Addie laid her head back down and he held her. Nick had never been one to cuddle much, but he loved having her so close that he could touch whenever he wanted. When her soft breaths slowed, he knew she was asleep and closed his eyes. But sleep didn't come to him easily. Tomorrow he was going to confront his stepfather, and he was terrified about it.

The dream, if that was what it was, started out slowly. He and Addie were in a limo. Nick had no idea where they were going, but the sudden appearance of his stepfather made him think this wasn't a normal nightmare.

"Hello, shit head." Nick held onto Addie, knowing for some reason Dane was there to get her. "I will, you know. Get her I mean. And when I do, you're going to do just what I tell you to do. Even going so far as killing that fucking killer."

"Who would that be? You? Gladly. Ellen Wooten? Again, I'd gladly kill her for you. And we will." Dane reached for him, but it was as if he'd been blocked. Even he looked surprised by his inability to touch him. "Any last requests, Dane? Like, I don't know, maybe you could have me tell Mom and Ana how sorry you were for ruining all our lives."

"You think I'm sorry for that? Nope. What I'm sorry about is that I'd not killed you when I had the chance. And I did, boy, and you know it." Dane leaned back on the seat, and that was when Nick saw his hand. It was burned. Right where he'd been blocked, his hand was burned badly. "You and me, we're going to have us some fun now. You just wait and see. And that woman of yours? I cannot wait to get me a piece of her too."

Nick felt a calmness settle over him just as he was ready to lash out at Dane. He had no idea how she was doing it, but he knew that it was Addie. Putting his hand over his heart, he felt her there. Not her hand but her love, and it calmed him more.

"You're not going to touch her. Do you want to know why?" Dane looked confused and Nick loved it. It was the first time in all his life that he wasn't afraid of the man. "Because I know how to beat you now. All of you. And we're going to."

"You think so?" Dane didn't sound so sure now. His voice, always so strong and loud, sounded slightly nervous to Nick. "We'll just see about that. But you know this. I'm going to get you here with me, and not a day won't go by that I don't fuck you in that pretty ass of yours like I used to."

"Never. Never again." Nick smiled. "Be gone from me while in this place." When he was gone, Nick closed his eyes again. He knew that for now, rest would come easy to him. And for the first time in longer than he could remember, Nick felt at peace with himself and the world.

Nick.

CHAPTER 12

The house looked like it had before. The yard was slightly more overgrown and there were still newspapers on the front porch, but so far as appearances went, it looked like no one had lived in this house for a long time.

Steele didn't move right into the yard. He wanted to wait, to see what he could find out before he did that. The police were itching to go in and take Ellen out, but he knew as sure as he was standing there that it would not end well for the police, no matter how many guns they had.

"She in there?" Steele looked over at Landon and the cop who had been following them around for the last hour. "He'd like to be able to send in the troops."

Steele didn't answer either man. Landon was pissed off. The cop was making them all nuts, and the cop had his hand on his gun like it was going to do him a bit of good on the rest of the monsters in the house. Instead of standing there and telling him again that they needed some answers first, he went to find their contact, Sergeant Perrier.

Madeline Perrier was the most laid back cop he'd ever worked with. Not only had she risen to the rank of sergeant in a relatively short amount of time, the townspeople in her little burg wanted her to run for mayor as well. Steele had no doubt that she'd do a fine job of that too.

"Steele? Everything all...?" She glanced over his shoulder, and he knew that the cop was hot on his heels. "He is going to shoot his fucking dick off if he doesn't calm now. I'll take care of him. Anything else I should know?"

"Billy and two more are looking inside. I'm waiting on them before we go in with our heads on a platter for her." She nodded and Wonder-Cop came up beside him. "When I have it, you'll have it."

"I was thinking that we should send in one of them drone things. You know, with a camera on it." Wonder-Cop smiled and started nodding as he continued. "My kid has one of them. Does a fine job of seeing all kinds of stuff in the room you normally wouldn't be privy to."

"What a fine idea." Both Steele and Wonder-Cop looked at Perrier when she spoke. "You go on back to the station and get ours. Tell Mavis that I said it was in the locked room in the sublevels of the jail. The box is marked tromper."

Steele watched the cop leave them, and he turned to Perrier. She was laughing pretty hard as she waved the moron away when he drove by them in a cruiser. He cleared his throat and looked at her.

"Tromper?" She nodded and told him what it meant. "Ah. So he doesn't speak French, I guess, and has no idea that you're telling Mavis that he's a fool."

"I'm pretty sure she knows that anyway, but it's code for her to keep him there for me. We've used this ploy before." Perrier shook her head. "I might take the mayoral job just to get away from fools like him."

Billy prevented him from telling her she should take it anyway. He looked...well, nauseous, Steele thought, and wondered what sort of things were going on in the house. Steele excused himself and walked to where the rest of his group was.

"She's been busy. I mean…Christ, you should see what she's been up to." Billy looked away, then back at them. "I never seen the likes of it, Steele. Never. But she's been taking out her frustrations on the men that she's lured there. Three of them I think. It's bad."

Steele had talked to the others, ghosts that were loyal to him, and had them working the yard. None of them had reported that anyone had gotten by them, but he knew that their way of doing things wasn't perfect. Three men. Steele asked him if that included the pizza boy that had come up missing a few days ago.

"I can't tell." Billy looked at Carlton, who had come to stand with them. Nick was on his cell phone and he could tell that he was upset, but he had no idea why. As Billy continued, Steele sent his sister to Nick. "The blood is just everywhere. She's been using the table in the kitchen as her lab, I think."

"There are four bodies in the house. All dead and all have been tortured not just by her, but by Glass's troops as well after they are dead. Steele, I have never seen such a bloodbath before. And the dead are needing to move on. They've suffered enough." Steele nodded and looked at the house as Carlton continued. "I've sent young Donny home. There is no reason for him to be here. He's…I know that he's been gone from this earth for a while, but he's much too young to see this."

Steele told him it was a good idea. And when his sister came back to him, Steel knew that something else had happened. Before she could tell him, however, Nick came to him. He looked like a man that had been run over.

"Evie is gone. Bentley was taking her around to houses and was in an accident. I don't...I'm not sure what happened yet, but Bentley was taken to the hospital and he is worried to death about Evie." Nick's phone rang again. "That's Addie. She was headed to the hospital with Kari, and I told her to call me when she got there."

Steele was afraid now. He had no idea if the accident had anything to do with what they were doing here, but he had a gut feeling that it didn't. He looked at Perrier and told her what was going on.

"I just heard. I'm sending out my best men now." Steele thanked her. "Do you think that the woman in there...you think she had anything to do with the accident and disappearance?"

"No. I don't know why, but I don't." She nodded, and her mike at her shoulder screamed some information at her. Steele let her walk away to deal with it and looked for Hugh. After telling him what had happened, Hugh said he'd go.

"I'll take Carlton with me, and Billy. Unless you think they can help you with this?" They couldn't, so Steele told him to take them. "I'll keep in touch. Just let me know what I can do if you need me."

By the time Hugh was gone, Nick seemed to calm. The man had been so different lately that he wondered if he knew why. Steele knew. It was love. It had the same affect—a thought occurred to him.

"Nick, where is Addie?" He told him she was on her way to the hospital. "Tell her to come here. I think...I have a feeling that I know what the book was telling us. And tell her to bring Kari. We're going to beat these odds right now."

It took them twenty minutes to get there. The more he thought about it, the more Steele thought it would work. Nick had two of his own friends go to the hospital to keep an eye on Bentley as the rest of them decided on a course of action. It was then that Aster came out of the house with an infant in her arms.

"They need help." Steele nodded and watched her return to the house only to come back with two more. They were tiny, much smaller than a newborn, and he knew they were the children that Summer had told them about. The third time she came back, Aster looked like she'd been crying. He asked her what it was. "She's found them. I'm not sure if one of Glass's men found them or she did. Ellen can see the others, so she might be able to see these little souls as well."

There were nine in all. Most of them were no bigger than the palm of his hand, but all of them had been hurt. Steele had never worked with someone so young before, and wasn't even sure how to proceed. But Aster came back to him with the last child, and he knew that he had to do something. This baby had been used up, was all he could think had happened to her. He picked up the first one and held it to his chest.

He saw it then…what had happened to it. The little boy had been the result of an abortion. The house, it seemed, had been used for illegal acts such as the one preformed on these children for months before someone had come in and killed the doctor. Steele looked at Ray when he came to stand beside him.

"Can you feel it?" Steele told him that he could. "That monster is trying to suck their energy out of them even from here. We have to send them on. Know how?"

"No. Do you?" Ray took the small child from him and held it up. Steele watched as he prayed, something he'd ever seen the man do before. Then when his wife, Betty Hancock, showed up, Steele realized it wasn't a prayer so much as a plea for help.

"Hello, darling." Steele watched them together. Ray and Betty had always been such a loving couple. Steele wished that he'd known her before she had died. He was sure she was even nicer back then. "I've come to help you. All of you. But the babies will need to be taken too."

"You can help them?" Betty looked at Steele and smiled. "Thank you, my lady. You have no idea what this means to me."

"You have been a very good boy, young Steele. We're all very proud of you." She turned and handed the child she'd taken from Ray to a woman behind her. "As soon as they're free of this place, we'll help you."

Once the babies were gone, all of them cradled in the arms of elderly women who were talking to them as they disappeared, Steele saw his own wife coming toward him. Kari was talking a mile a minute to Addie, but stopped and looked at him when he softly said her name, as if she might have heard him. When she leapt into his arms, Steele held her to him. This was his world.

"I was just telling Addie that her grandmother is fine. If she wasn't you'd know it." He looked at the other woman who was being held by Nick. "You haven't heard from her, have you? I mean, she's still with us, right?"

"I've not heard from her." Kari nodded and put her head on his shoulder. "We have to finish this, and you and Addie are going to help us. I have a plan."

"I'm sure you do." Her giggle told him that she was joking with him, but he also knew that she trusted him. He told her and Addie what the plan was and they both nodded. He just hoped this worked.

~~~

Addie knew that she was holding onto Nick's hand much too tightly, but she was terrified. Not for being where she was but for her grandmother. To come all this way in her life, only to have this happen to her the moment that the two of them were about to embark on their lives as a family. Whoever did this was certainly going to pay when she found them.

"Well, well, well. Look who the fucking bastard brought me." She turned and looked in the direction of the voice. Addie had to concentrate hard on bringing him into focus, and once she did, she gripped Nick's hand all the tighter. She thought perhaps it was the screwdriver that was sticking in his head that gave her strength, but she was sure that Kari and Steele coming into the room with her helped too. "Real nice of him to bring you to me so I don't gotta go out and bring you here. Damn, but you're a fine piece of ass."

"And you're just an asshole." When he stood up, Addie lifted her chin at the man. It was then that she realized how small he was. Not just short, but small. And mean. "You're nothing to me. And Nick and I have each other now, so you're nothing to him either."

"You think so? I bet I can still make him wet his pants. Did he tell you that? That I'd only have to come into his room to get him and he'd piss himself? Big baby." She laughed and Dane smiled. "You want more stories about that lover of yours and I got them. Got me a whole mess of them."

"When you came into his room to rape him, you mean? Or would it have been when you came for his sister?"

Addie had no idea where her strength to stand up to this man was coming from, but she felt empowered by it. "I really think you should just back off. You're not going to get to him anymore. Not so long as I'm around."

"We can take care of that for you. I'd like nothing better than to take you down to my little fun shop and cut you up. Did you know that I've had nobody here to play with for so long? Dane tells me it's because somebody has been very naughty. Was it you?" Addie turned and looked at the woman who spoke. "Oh yeah, you're going to be fun. I bet you'll hold out until the very end without screaming. But I have news for you, they all scream in the end."

"There will be no screaming today. At least not any from us. As for your victims not coming around, that would be because of me." Several of the ghosts backed up when Steele spoke. For such a young man, she realized how much power he had. When he lifted his hand up to his mouth—the one curled around Kari's hand—and kissed it, several of the other ghosts screamed. "You aren't going to like what I have to say to you, Ellen Margaret Wooten."

Ellen cringed from him. Steele didn't move, but Addie could swear that he got bigger, the glow around him got just a little brighter. When a noise to her right made her turn, Addie looked at Dane just as he reached for Nick.

"I don't think so." Addie felt herself being pulled back to Nick. A strong force seemed to be sucking her to Dane, and Nick pulled her back. As he looked at his stepfather, Addie could see a newfound calmness in Nick. He didn't seem to be as terrified of him as he had in their dreams. She knew it was true when he spoke to Dane again. "I have no idea why I've let you rule my life. But it ends here. I have a life, a love, and I'm not going to let you rule it again."

"You think so?" Nick laughed and nodded at Dane. "Well, I'm the fucking boss of you, you fucking moron, and what I say goes. I got me a good crew now and we're going to bring you to our side."

"No. No...you're not going to do that." Joel stepped in front of her and Nick and put his arms over his chest. Joel looked right at Dane as he continued. "I've been out looking for my own crew. And I've...so you know, I'm not going to take your shit any more either."

"You think.... You sure have grown a couple since you ran away." Dane turned to the three men left and laughed. The others, the only men left in what had been a group of ten, looked like they were ready to bolt too. "Ain't he the shit? Here he is telling me what he thinks he's going to do. We got us something new for him, don't we? Show him boys."

None of them moved. Even when Dane turned to tell them to get Nick, they backed up, getting as much distance between them and Nick as they could. Laughing at the man, Nick turned to his stepfather. Addie felt the power of something move over her and realized that someone...something...had moved into her.

"Hello, Dane." The voice was hers, but Addie knew that it wasn't her speaking. The woman...child really...was speaking to Dane through her. "I've been looking for you. Did you know that Mother and I have been left behind because of you?"

"Who the hell are you?" The voice laughed, bitter and cold, and Dane took a step back. "No. No, that ain't right. You're not supposed to be able to break free of that shit. You're dead 'cause you killed yourself."

"No. I'm dead because you left me no choice. There was no one left for me to turn to. You told me that my brother was dead." Addie and the child walked toward Dane. "You lied to me, Dane. Just like you always did, but this time you did it as a ghost, and that just doesn't work the same way."

Dane backed up and Ana—she knew who she was now—looked at Nick. Tears in her eyes, she reached for her brother using Addie, and the moment they touched, she could feel everything Ana had as a child when she'd been told her brother had died. When she turned to Dane again, the power that came from her shot out and touched the other men behind him before hitting Dane. They were all gone in seconds. Ana turned her to Nick.

"I'm sorry." Addie touched her fingers to Nick's cheek just as Ana wanted. "Mother and I are at peace now. You will be happy and free of him. He is gone."

"I'm sorry, Ana. Don't go." She turned and Addie could see the shadow of the woman just beyond them. "Mom?"

"We have to go." Ana turned to him. "The woman, kill her. If you don't, then she will live to haunt others."

"I will." Nick reached for her again. "I've missed you. I'm so sorry. I didn't have any idea where to find you."

"It's good, Nicky. We had a job to do and now that it's done, we're going to be just fine. And so are you." Addie felt the warmth from the child as she left her body. When she turned to her, Addie could see her just as clearly as if she were standing right in front of her. "You will help him, yes?"

"I love him." Nodding, Ana smiled at her. "I wish I could have known you. Both of you. I'm sorry for what happened to you all."

"You will know us. Through him." Turning again to Nick, Ana told him again to kill the woman. "Do not let her go to prison again. She will survive."

"We'll take care of her."

When Ana faded away, Addie looked at Ellen. She was having a heated argument with Steele, and Addie knew that Ana was right. If she lived, she'd get out and kill again. It had to stop now.

The officer that came into the house looked confused. Addie had no idea what he was talking about as he mumbled about head pain and a woman. But as soon as he was within touching distance of Ellen, she grabbed him around the chest and pulled him to her. The knife was at his throat before anyone could move. Addie moved to help him, but only managed to fall against him. She was kicked back before she could stand again.

"This is how this is going to work. You four are going to get out of my house and leave me alone. And if you do what I say, then I'll let this guy go." Her laughter made Addie think that Ellen had no such intentions of letting anyone go, not even them. "And those cops out there, they're going to leave too. I've got work to do."

"You're insane." Addie felt her face heat when she realized what she'd said. But Ellen nodded at her and smiled. "That's the plan, isn't it? You're going to tell them that you're insane and get sent back to prison."

"It wasn't prison. It was a home." Ellen licked the officer's face, and Addie looked at him. He had no idea what was going on, but Addie did. As she stood up, she felt it in her hand before she could think what it was, much less how it had gotten there. Lifting the gun up, Addie pointed it at Ellen and watched her face.

"Let him go." Ellen laughed again, manically and full of insanity. "I said to let him go and I won't kill you."

"You won't kill me anyway. You're just too sweet for that." Ellen spit at her. "Fuck you and your sweetness. I'm going to enjoy cutting him to shit. Then I'm coming for you. When I get you, you're going to scream like you've never screamed before. See that—"

The gun seemed to just fire itself. Addie held it up even as Ellen's head snapped back. The officer that had been in her arms fell to the floor and held his neck. Addie watched as Ellen stared at her, not a drop of blood coming from the neat hole that was right between her eyes. As she dropped to her knees, then to the floor, Steele was taking the gun from her, and Addie just stared at him when he said her name again.

"Let me have it, Addie." Nodding, she stared at the gun. "Addie, you have to let go, honey. If you won't give it to me, then give it to Nick."

"I can't." Nick was suddenly in front of her. "My fingers won't loosen up. Help me. I want to let go, but I can't."

"I've got you." His fingers peeled hers away, and she felt like she was another person watching it happen. "Addie, look at me, not at her."

It was then that she realized that she was staring at the body. Her mind was fuzzy on a few things. Like when did the sheet get put over Ellen? Where did the police officer go? How long had she been sitting in this chair? Nick said her name and she looked at him again. There was blood on his face, but she couldn't seem to lift her arms to wipe it away.

"Can you hear me?" Nodding made her sick, so she answered him instead. "Can you see her? Can you see Ellen now, baby? Tell me what you see."

Addie looked at the body. Nick told her no, Ellen's ghost. Looking around the room, she saw her then. Ellen was being held by Ana and another woman. It was Summer…she was there as well.

"Yes. She's being taken away." As she watched, not only was Ellen being pulled by the women, each of them at one arm and one leg, but another person, a male, was there as well, helping the women as they continued to pull her along. "They're pulling her apart. Tearing her limb from limb."

Addie giggled then, the sound of it kind of scary. Then the man turned to her, the man that had just pulled Ellen's leg free from her body. It was Joel. Joel was helping them take care of Ellen, and she told Nick everything as she was overwhelmed by it all.

Nick held her while the police asked questions. The body, the shell that had been Ellen, was still in the house, but she knew that she'd never bother anyone again. Addie was asked about the gun, why she'd killed Ellen, and a few other things. Addie answered all their questions, but said nothing of the ghosts that were there with them. All of them were speaking to her, and she understood.

As they were leaving the house, Addie went to find Steele. He and Kari were holding one another, and she asked to speak to him alone. There were several things she wanted…no needed, to tell him, and if he was mad at her, she didn't want to be embarrassed.

"They said I was like you." Steele nodded, not saying a word. "I'm to help you in ways that no one else can. That since…since I've been chosen to help you, my children will be able to do this too."

"That's what I heard too." He looked around. "Kari knows. She said you need to tell Nick. He's going to be afraid for you for a while."

"I love him." Steele put his arm around her and kissed her on the forehead. "What was that for?"

"Because, my dear necromancer, I love you as well."

CHAPTER 13

"They're all gone." Nick knew that without Steele having to tell him, but to be honest, he was really glad to hear it from someone else. "And we have a lead on Evie. She's being held in her daughter's home. Addie seems to think that her mother has gone off the deep end. Donny found her for us."

Donny had told him first that he'd found her. He even told him to make sure that Addie knew he'd done it. There was some fear there, and Nick hoped that his young friend would get over it soon. Nick had called Benson the moment he'd learned where Evie was.

"I'd say it has to do more with the money than anything else. Did you talk to Bentley?" Steele said that he had. "The poor man is beside himself with worry. He's terrified that she'll be killed before he can tell her how much he's loved her."

"She's in good hands." Which Nick also knew, but only nodded at his friend. "Addie is...she said she was going there. I don't think that's a good idea. She's too...raw, I guess."

She was too. Addie had been hiding in their bedroom since the police had released her from the shooting. Nick had a feeling that Steele had had a lot to do with the reason she'd not seen any jail time. As soon as an hour after the shooting, Addie was going home with him.

"The others, the ghosts, are driving her a little nutty. They want to work for her." Steele nodded. "I don't know how to help her with that. She's seeing more than I can."

"She sees what I do now. And I'm trying to help her with it. But it's just too much." Steele had been like this his whole life, Nick knew, so he'd needed very little in the way of adjustments. Addie was simply overwhelmed. "She's getting better, but it might take her a bit."

"Do you know why she is like you?" Nick wasn't jealous about what Addie could do. He was very proud of her, as a matter of fact. But he was concerned. This was a lot to hang on one person. Especially one that, up until a few weeks ago, hadn't even believed in ghosts. "She said they only told her that she'd be helpful to you and that you'd be the same. No explanations, just that."

"It's because of that that she's been picked to help me. They seem to think that with her help, they can use us more." Steele only laughed. "I think it's great. I'm looking forward to the help."

Not too long ago, Steele had decided to give up helping the dead. He hated it, he'd told Nick, telling him that because of them, he'd been angry with his sister the morning that she was killed. He also blamed them for him not being there when she needed him. Now, and Nick supposed it was because of Kari, not only was he helping them more, but he was stronger as well, and much more relaxed. Nick thought he was as well.

As they loaded in the car an hour later, Nick thought about what they were about to do. He had no idea how much Addie was worth, didn't really care, but he knew from the conversation he'd had with her lawyer that Addie was worth a great deal. When they pulled up in front of the house that she'd grown up in after their short drive, he stared at it before turning to her.

"How much?" She frowned at him and he looked at the house before continuing. "This is about twice the size of Steele's house. So either this is a hotel with several hundred more people in it than are at the Grand Hotel, or you're worth a good deal more than him."

"It's not mine. What I had when you found me is all I have." He nodded and grabbed her arm when she started to get out of the car. "My parents are going to inherit the money, Nick. Grandma is very wealthy, sure, but I already told her that I don't want it. I'm happy with what she's already given me."

Nick let her go and thought perhaps he might get an answer from Evie. He also thought that Evie had her own plans when it came to her money, thus the reason for her being kidnapped from her own car. As they entered the house with Benson, Nick had a feeling that there was a great deal going on behind these closed doors other then what poor Evie had stirred up when she'd left her home.

"What is the meaning of this?" A very well dressed man met them in the grand hall when their coats were taken. He was standing there like he had no idea who they were, when Nick knew for a fact that he'd been told they were coming. "Benson, what have you done? This is my home, not a show house for you to bring every person you know off the streets."

"I didn't tell him." It took a few moments for what Benson whispered to him to sink in. Then Benson walked toward Mr. West. When he turned to the man, he introduced him to Nick, but not Addie. "Mr. West, I did tell you I was bringing a couple with me to use as witnesses. These are my witnesses. Where is Mrs. Simon-English? You said that she would be here."

"I'm here, Benson. Hello Nick. Darling." Addie nodded to her grandmother, who had been put in a wheelchair. Nick would bet anything that she was tied to it rather than in need of it. When he leaned down to kiss her cheek, she showed him that not only was she tied to the thing, but she'd been hurt too. Her arm was bruised badly. "So, we're going to do this the hard way, are we? I don't know why you think the presence of Benson is going to make me sign things, but you always were stupid, Dalton."

"You'll do as you're told, or so help me, I'll have you declared unfit to live alone and have you shoved into a nursing home. The worst in the state. You'll sign them now, Evangeline, or else." Evie winked at him. "Benson, I do hope you've briefed them on what is going on here. I don't have time for this nonsense. Addison has taken to her bed, she's so upset. She had to miss her garden meeting when all this came out. And I don't think they're going to be having her back. She is most annoyed with this."

"Poor Mother. Whatever will she do without her garden club? Do they still have those meetings at the country club, Father? I bet missing out on all that free liquor has really put a damper in her day." Dalton stared at Addie as if he had no idea who she was. Addie must have seen his look, because she laughed before speaking again. "Don't you know me, Father? I'm your daughter. Your long lost daughter, Addie West."

"I have no daughter." He turned his back on her and glared at Benson. "Is this your idea of a joke, Benson? If so, I'm not finding it particularly funny. Get her out of here. I've told you before, she's not ever welcome here."

"I can't throw her from her own house, Dalton. Not even you can have that done." Benson left them standing there and moved to the wheelchair. "How have you been, Mrs. E.? I do hope that they've treated you with some respect."

Benson pulled out a small knife and cut the ropes at her arms. As he cut her legs loose from the chair, Nick held her hand to help with the circulation that seemed to be painful to her small hands. Addie came over to her grandmother and kissed her cheek as he helped Evie from the chair.

"What the hell are you doing? If you don't tie her back up, I'm going to call the authorities." Dalton started for them, and Nick stepped in front of him. "Young man, you don't want to screw with me. I'm a very wealthy man. And you look as if you don't have a pot to piss in."

"Oh, Dalton, stop being such a bore." Evie led the way to another room with the help of Addie. "Come along, the rest of you. I'm tired and in need of a long bath. Oh, Addie, how is Bentley? That monster over there had him hurt in that accident. Imagine hitting our car to have me brought here to be treated like an animal."

"He's fine, Grandmother. Just fine. He has a broken leg, but the doctor said that he'd heal nicely with time. Steele has gotten him a nurse to care for him and to pamper him endlessly. Also, you should see—"

"Shut up." Everyone looked at Dalton, and Evie cocked a brow at him. The man was ruddy with his anger, and he glared back at Evie as he continued. "Don't give me that look. You know as well as I do that you've brought this on all by yourself. What the hell did you expect me to do when you literally kicked me from my home? And had my credit cards cut up like I was nothing more than...well, than a common criminal?"

"You are a common criminal, you moron. Ah, there she is. My darling daughter, Addison the first. How are you, child? Drunk yet?"

Nick watched the woman stagger into the room and sit on the couch that was nearest to Dalton. She was Addie's mother, there was no doubt about that, but looks were as far as the resemblance went. Addie was nothing like her mother.

"What do you think of your daughter, Addison? Didn't she turn out well?"

"I have had this conversation with you before, Mother. Addison was no longer my child the moment she embarrassed us by leaving in the middle of the night." Nick watched the elder Addison ignore her daughter. "I do hope that this ridiculous mess is cleared up now. I have a hair appointment tomorrow, and I should hate to have to cancel it. The last time I was there, my cards were taken from me. Mother, you'll have to take care that that doesn't happen again. Just sign the papers and we'll all pretend that this didn't happen."

"I can't help you there, Addison. I'm broke."

If Nick hadn't been looking at Dalton, he might have missed the look in his face. Terror along with disbelief. When he recovered a little, he looked at Benson, who nodded at him.

"My house has been sold as well. And this house has a new owner too. So the sooner you move out, the sooner the new owners can move in. I do believe they might want to do some updating on the house. Frankly, I'd just gut the place and start over, but that's just me."

"You can't have sold our home. It's ours." Benson told Dalton that it wasn't and never had been. "We've owned this house since we were married. You said it was a wedding present. You even told me that you hoped that I'd fill it with children so that they could live here long after we were gone."

"But you never fulfilled your end of the bargain, did you? And when you didn't, my father had you sign the deed over to Jacob when he was alive. Then you nearly lost it when you didn't pay the taxes for the first ten years." Benson tried to hand Dalton a file. "It's all right here, Dalton. You defaulted on the taxes, therefore having the house revert to its original owner. And since Jacob is gone, Mrs. E. owned it, lock, stock, and smoking gun."

"Taxes? Why should I have to pay taxes on a gift? And you never said anything about taxes when you gave us the house." A sheet of paper was pulled from the file and handed to Dalton. Even from where he was, Nick could see it was a contract. "I'm not going to say this again, Evie; sign the papers and let's have this done with. I'm not in the mood for your childish behavior any longer."

"I told you, Dalton, I'm broke. I've signed everything over, and I only own what I have in my bank account right now." Nick nearly laughed. He'd bet anything that there was more in her bank account than most people made in their entire lives. When Evie winked at him, Nick had a feeling she knew what he was thinking. "If I were you, I'd not mess around with this. Get out before the newspaper is called and let in on your dirty little secret."

"What are you talking about? I have nothing to hide." But he did, and Nick thought that he knew it too. "I've changed my mind. I'm just going to let the courts deal with you. But I warn you, I'm not going to be as nice as —"

"It's my house." Addie had been so quiet until then that he'd nearly forgotten she was a part of all this. "The house, the money, all if it...it's mine, isn't it, Grandmother?"

"It is. When I heard from Nick here, I had Benson change everything to your name. It was my intention all along to leave it all to you, but I thought I'd have so much more fun if I could actually see your father's face when he found out." Evie laughed. "It was worth it. Dalton, I'd like for you to meet the new homeowners. Like I said, I'd not mess with her. She's a good deal stronger than you'll ever be. Oh, and so you're aware, you've been booted off the board at West Iron Works as well. They never really cared for you much after my husband left the company anyway."

Dalton sat down and stared at his daughter. Nick was sure that his mind was going a mile a minute. He'd bet anything that he was trying to figure out how to make this new predicament work in his favor. When Dalton looked at his wife, Nick took Addie's hand. He was sure it was going to be horrible, whatever spilled from his mouth.

"This is all your fault. I told you from the start that children were never going to give us anything but trouble. But you found yourself pregnant and you just had to keep it. Now look. She's our landlord." Addie laughed and he glared at her before continuing with his wife. "You brought her into this world, and now you're going to deal with her. Get this settled now, Addison. I want things the way they were as soon as possible."

~~~

When her dad stood up and went to the fireplace, Addie looked at him. He'd not aged a day since she'd left here, and she'd bet it was due more to a surgeon's knife rather than any clean living or exercise on his part. Her mother too. She still had the same blonde hair she'd had as a teenager, and a figure that looked like she'd starved herself for months instead of being healthy and active. Neither of them had even played a round of golf so far as she knew, even though they were members of the country club that boasted a fine tennis court as well as beautiful golf course. She moved to stand in front of him, but he looked away.

"Look at me, Father." Addie tried twice to stand in her father's view, but he refused to see her. "I have never meant anything to either of you, have I?"

"You were a nuisance your entire life. Had it not been for the help here, I might have sent you away. But Mother forbade it." Addie turned to her mom when she spoke. "Her paying off my debt to…well, her paying things off for me and Dalton saved us a bit of embarrassment, so we had to keep you once she put it in the paper that you were born. After that…well, we sort of forgot about you unless someone reminded us."

Her mom glared at her grandmother. She wasn't wanted. Not by the two people in the world that had brought her into it. Sitting down, she stared at her mom, then her father. It was time to fix this. And she was past caring how they felt about it. Turning to Benson, she smiled at him.

"Since they don't want to deal with me, I'll have to work through you. I want them gone by the end of the month. Everything that is theirs and not my grandmother's gift, I want it out of here too." Benson told her that Evie had purchased it all, because she'd paid the credit off monthly when it was ordered. "Then get rid of it all. I don't care if you have to put it all out on the lawn and have a tag sale, get rid of it."

"You will do no such thing." Her father roared at her, and she stood up. "This is no way to treat me. You've no rights to this money. Your mother should get it all. I want nothing to do with you. So far as I'm concerned, you do not exist."

"Oh, but I do, and you will have to deal with me. And as for you not wanting anything to do with me, that's perfect because I want nothing to do with you either when this is over."

He drew back his hand to no doubt hit her, but he never got the chance. Nick had him pinned to the wall even before his arm was cocked all the way back.

"Get out. Right now, get out before I call the police."

"You will have respect for me, or so help me, I will ruin you." She laughed at him. "Addison West, you're to end this right now. I'll...I'll even see a way to letting you come to visit us when it's a good time if you just do as you're told."

"I'm done doing what I'm told. As of right now, I have no parents." She turned to Milly, the household cook and good friend. "Call the police, please? There are intruders in the house."

When she left to do as she was asked, Addie turned to her mother. She sat there looking at Addie like she wanted to murder her. Her father looked at her no differently. Addie asked Nick to let her father go, and Addie watched as he straightened his suit and tie before addressing her.

"Now. This is the way we're going to do this. Milly will not be calling the police, and if she has, then this is what you're going to tell them. That you've only just gotten here after...after you've been kidnapped for so long and you were frightened. That will play nicely for the papers. You'll, of course, have to stay in a nice facility for a time, just to make sure that you're well. Then after that, you'll live with someone who will care for you until such time as arrangements can be made for you to be out in the public again." Addie shook her head. "Addison, I'm not going to put up with this any longer. You'll do as you're told for once in your life."

"I'm going to live here. In my house, with my husband." Addie took Nick's hand when he put it out for her. "You will live where you want. How you want, and you will have to find a job, I guess."

"Addison, what is wrong with you?" Addie turned to her mother, and her smile made Addie feel dirty and nasty. "This is not the way we do things. We're Wests, and Wests do not marry the first man that comes along. If you insist on getting married after a time, we'll find someone for you. Benson, darling, put out the word now that we're in the market for a husband for Addison. He'll have to be older than her. Someone that is established, and he must have his own money. We're not parting with ours now that we have it back."

Addie moved to the door, taking Nick with her. She was nearly to it when she heard the sirens. Her grandmother was right behind them when she opened the door for the police. This was going to be hard on her, she knew it. On both of them, she supposed. It was her mom and her grandmother's daughter, but enough was enough. Smiling to the first officer in the door, she told him what was going on.

Within two hours, her parents were being led out of the house and into a waiting cab. Closing the door behind them, she leaned against it and cried. The strong arms around her had her turning into Nick's chest and sobbing out her pain.

It took her an hour to settle the house. Most of the staff were glad to have her parents gone, and the few that weren't were out the door almost as fast as her parents had been. She looked at the remaining staff and then at the house. Benson had told her that everything was taken care of, that all she had to do was sign the deed and the paperwork that would make her the richest woman in the world.

"There will be a great many changes." May, who had been hiding in the other room until her parents had left, told her good. "Not all of them will be good, I'm afraid. Most will, I hope, but there will be some bumps in the road. I've never taken care of a house before."

"We'll help you." May patted her on the back as she moved toward the telephone and picked it up. "I'm going to order pizzas. I've not had that many, and I'm finding that I've no energy to cook tonight."

The entire staff sat in the dining room while Benson told them what was going to happen. The garage sale was going to be a little lighter because Nick and Addie agreed to let the staff have what they wanted of the household furniture, as she and Nick were going to start anew. Things were already looking up.

Her grandmother was in the living room just after things were cleaned up and Addie went to sit with her.

"I'm very proud of you." Addie kissed her on the cheek and hugged her to her. "I just spoke to Bentley. He said to tell you that he's proud of you as well."

"I talked to him before coming here. I've asked him to live with us. He said that only if it was your desire. I'm hoping that you'll say yes." Her grandmother looked in the corner of the room and Addie did as well. "Grandda is there. I can see him."

"I see him too. He told me that I'm going to be here awhile yet." Addie felt her heart twist and she asked her what she meant. "I thought that now that you're all settled that I'd just go and see him. But he said no. I have things to do here."

"I should hope so. I know nothing about being the rich and famous." Her grandmother smiled. "You can't leave me, I need you. You're all I have in the world."

"You have Nick." Addie nodded, but it wasn't the same, she told her grandmother. "He's in love with you. I've never seen a love like he has for you. Reminds me of my Jacob."

"I love him too. He told me that even though he thinks that you're an odd old bird, he loves you a great deal." Her grandmother smiled. "Please say you'll live with us. I really do need you. I have to learn how to be a West again."

"You were never a West. And you shouldn't want to be. You should be a Stark. That young man in there has a good solid name, and you'll do well to use it." Her grandmother took her hand in hers before continuing. "I'll stay for a time. But the moment you get tired of me, I want to know. You can just kick me to the curb, all right?"

"I can live with that." But they both were never going to be kicking anyone to the curb. Addie had her family back.

CHAPTER 14

"You should find you a woman and settle down. You're much too young to be talking to an old woman like me." Mitch snorted. He really did love this woman, and had she or even he been born in a different time, he'd have married her. Connie was one hell of a woman, ghost or not. "There has to be someone out there, younger, living, that you could be with."

"There more than likely is, but I don't want anyone else. You're perfect." She mumbled something about her being dead, that was what appealed to him, and he looked away.

"I'm sorry." Mitch waved her off. "But you really do need someone in your life, Mitch. And you need to talk to Steele. He needs to know that you're being sued."

"I don't have anything for them to take from me, and if he knew, he'd just step in and pay them off. There isn't any reason for them to be suing me, but he'd do it anyway." He sometimes wished that Connie wasn't so easy to talk to. Like when he'd told her about the lawyer. "I think being sued by a foster parent because I ran away from their home and had the nerve to tell the authorities I was gone is just stupid. If they wanted me to stay, then maybe they shouldn't have beat me."

It was more than that. It was a great deal more than that. He'd been abandoned at a very young age, and had been shuffled around from home to home for a long time after that. They would figure out that he was a little on the odd side—Mitch supposed talking to ghosts wasn't the norm—and then they'd kick him out. He'd even gone so far as to try to ignore the people who came to see him, and that hadn't worked out well either. His life had been shit since he'd been dropped off at the neighbor's house for a few hours and his parents never returned. Sometimes he wished that Ray had never pulled him from that box all that time ago to help him out.

"Mitch?" He looked up when his name was called from the house. Standing up, he waved at Kari, and then leaned against the fence railing that surrounded the cemetery. He had been debating for days if he should tell Connie or not, and now he supposed it was time.

"I'm leaving in a few days." She asked him where he was going. "I was thinking New York. At least for a few weeks or so. Then…I don't know after that. I just need to get away. And I figured this was as good a time as any."

"Why?" He had hoped that she'd not ask him that, but when she did, he just looked beyond where they were. "Mitch Riley, you tell me where you're going right this minute."

"I'm not very useful here, and I need a break." He looked at her then. Dawning and understanding seemed to come over her face at the same time. "I just need a break."

"And this other thing? With the lawsuit? What will you do about it? If you go now, Steele will find out, and he won't be happy that you didn't let him know." He knew that. And was trying to think of a way to tell him without sounding like a complete fool. "Please, just tell him."

"I've never had money. I do now, of course, but I don't know what to do with it. I don't need a lot. Steele won't take money for rent, and everything else—food and heat, and even transportation I need—he provides for me as well." He was trying to get to the point, but he'd lost his way somehow. Smiling, he looked at Connie and remembered. "I'm going to tell him to use what he needs, I guess. I will take a little of what I have—there is about a hundred grand in the account—but wherever I go, I can make do with what I have or get a job."

"You're not going to be happy doing that. We both know that. You love helping people like us." He did to a point, but like he'd told her, he needed a break. "Here he comes. Tell him now."

Steele was walking toward him. He knew that the man came here a few times a week now and just sat by the graves. Mitch knew that he visited his father's grave as well. Not often, but he'd go there when he was really frustrated and more than likely would tell the man how much he hated him. The closer Steele got to him, the more Mitch could tell he was upset.

"She's gone." Mitch didn't have to ask him who. Eloise Bennett, the woman who had claimed to be his mother for most of his life, had died. "Kari said I should have her buried near my father. I think she might be right."

Mitch said nothing, but watched as Connie left them alone. Steele and his parents were the worst kind of family. And the hatred between Eloise and him had been horrendous. Mitch waited for him to say more before he asked what he really wanted to know.

"Yes." Mitch looked at Steele when he spoke. "You're going to ask me, and I'm telling you yes, Aster was there when she died. She swears to me that she had nothing to do with it, but I don't know if I believe her. Not that she doesn't have a damned good reason for wanting her dead...both of us do. But I don't know if she talked her into it or not."

"If she said that she didn't, then she didn't." Steele leaned against the railing like he was. Mitch was all right with the silence and so was Steele. They were the other two of the group that could sit in a room together and never say much more than a dozen words for hours on end. And they were comfortable with it.

"Do you know a person by the name of Vinnie Graham?" Mitch stiffened. Yes, he knew the name. It was the attorney who was trying to contact him about the lawsuit. "I got a letter from them today. Apparently, you're being sued by a man by the name of Mark Bruce."

"I was going to tell you eventually." Steele said nothing, and Mitch decided it was time, more than likely past time. "I left their household when I was fifteen. Ten years ago I guess. There were some problems, some of it mine, mostly theirs. But when I left them, I called the agency and told them that I'd had enough. That I was no longer living with them and wouldn't. That, I guess, stirred up a shit storm, and they were investigated. I don't think anything ever came of it, but they did figure out that not only was I gone from their care, but two others. The state took their money away from them, as well as demanded a refund on the money they'd been paid. Now, it seems that they think that I did them wrong, and they want me to pay them for pain and suffering."

"Did you? Suffer I mean?" Mitch didn't answer Steele, but he must have figured it out. "And how much do they want for their pain and suffering after ten years?"

"Five million." Steele whistled and stood up. Mitch did as well and they both started for the house. "I don't have that kind of money. And even if I did, I wouldn't give it to them. Not even as a settlement."

They were about fifty feet from the house when Steele spoke again, "She's here. Vinnie Graham. Showed up right before I went out to get you."

"She?" Steele nodded. "I don't want to talk to her. What the hell is she doing here? Trying to figure out if you can pay the debt for me?"

"She's not representing the Bruces. Miss Graham wants to represent you." Mitch stopped moving, and Steele had to stop and turn to look back at him. "Are you coming in to talk to her? And before you tell me no, I've had her looked into. Not for this, but for something…she wants to join my staff. And I guess she figured if she did a good job for you, I'd hire her."

"So I'm her test subject." Steele just stared at him. "I'm not going to dignify this lawsuit with a response. And hiring her will tell them that I have the money and can pay them."

"If you say so." Mitch loved Steele to death, but there were times, like right now, that he wanted to bash his head in. "She's not human."

"So?" Steele shrugged and started walking to the house again. "What is she, Steele? Another ghost? How will that work out for me? Having to relay everything she says so I can be made to look a fool again to these people."

"She's a vampire, and I doubt very much she will need you for much of anything to be honest. I'd say she's about three, maybe four hundred years old. I guess she's been studying law since before either of us were even thought of." He turned to him again just before going in the kitchen door. "Come inside and talk to her. And before you go off halfcocked, you should know that she has a...I guess you would call it her familiar. Someone that helps her during the day. He's very protective of her, so behave."

Mitch felt his temper rise up. He hated vampires. They were usually very cruel because of their boredom with life, and they tended to be slightly condescending. Most of the time. The few that he'd had to deal with over his lifetime had left him feeling dirty and pissy. And not that any of them had ever bitten him, but he still didn't like any of them. This woman with her familiar wasn't going to be getting any job with Steele either, if he had any say in it.

Mitch knew that he had a chip on his shoulder when he entered the living room. And seeing Kari and Addie sitting there with her didn't make his mood any better. How dare her suck up to the household like that? When the man stood up Mitch ignored him, but did note that he was flipping huge. Walking to who he assumed was Miss Graham, he started telling her what was what.

"I don't want you to help me out. I've decided that I'm just going to ignore this thing and hope for the best. I don't have that kind of money, and to think that I'd pay it to them for what they did to me is just ludicrous. To think that they're suing me when it should be the—"

"Mr. Riley, that's not me." He turned at the sound of the voice and then looked back at the woman he'd been blasting. "Yeah, that's my secretary. I'm Vinnie Graham."

~~~

Vinnie watched his face. She could see that he was pissed off. About what, she had a good idea at the moment, but the way he had come into the room like he owned it made her think it was less about the lawsuit and more about her—a vampire. She'd heard from Gilda, her secretary, that Mr. Riley did not play well with others, and not at all with vampires. Vinnie hoped that that part might have been wrong. Apparently not.

"You're very beautiful." Both of them flushed, and he looked away from her. "But be that as it may, Miss Graham, I will not need your services now or in the future."

"They're not going to go away. And neither will I. There are more than just you in this suit, Mr. Riley. They've named nineteen people in this stupidity. And if only one of you lose to them, they will go after more stupid claims." He turned and looked at her, and Vinnie could see that he was getting madder by the second. "I can go away, leave you to whatever it is you do, but they're going to come at you. And if they can't get it from you, they'll sue Mr. Bennett here."

"They're working on that now." Vinnie glanced at Steele when he spoke, but she watched Mitch. "They contacted my firm this morning, saying that I'm harboring you and they want their money. I'm not entirely sure what they think that means, but I'm sure that their lawyer will explain. I have a meeting with them next week."

"You can't be serious. Why are they going after you?" Vinnie started to tell Mitch why, but he answered his own question. "I see. You're the rich and powerful Steele Bennett, right? Will they go after Addie next? Or her grandmother?"

"I'm sure that they have." Mitch looked at her again. "This isn't going to go away. Newspapers have picked it up. A television crew was at their home just last week, and was showing how much they've suffered because of the way you and the others as children have done them wrong."

"We did them wrong? Do you have any idea what we had to suffer living there? The things that we had to do for a single meal a day?" She said nothing, and Mitch started pacing. The man could say more in one step than most people said in a whole conversation. "I ran away. I was only there for less than a year. And in that time...in that time I was treated with such atrocities that would...it was not a safe place for a child, much less a bunch of us."

When Gilda stood up, Vinnie shook her head at her. She knew things too. Things that had happened to this young man that should never have happened to an adult, much less a child. When she sat down, Vinnie looked at Hugo. He nodded once and picked up her briefcase, as well as her coat. If he wouldn't help her, then there was nothing much more she could do to make him. As they made their way to the door, Hugo stepped in front of her when someone, or something. moved beside her.

"She wants to know if you're related to Mr. Douglas Graham." Vinnie grabbed the back of the chair she was standing next to and nodded at Mitch. "She said that she's glad that you're no longer with him, but she wants to know if you killed him or did he get caught at something?"

"He was staked. About ten years ago." Vinnie looked around but saw no one. But she could feel it. A presence that she'd felt before since coming into this house. "Who's there?"

"She said that it's not important right now. And you should know that you brought her here with you." Mitch sat in the chair across from her and stared at something to her immediate left. "The woman is older, about sixtyish, I'd say. Dark hair and wearing a dress from about the turn of the century. I'd say she's been gone for about fifty years."

Vinnie moved around the chair then and sat down. She could feel Hugo there. He would never leave her, but Gilda was standing back. If this was who she thought it was, then Gilda would be in danger. All of them would be.

"Her name...ask her if she's Millicent. I don't know if I ever knew her last name." Mitch nodded. "I see. And you can speak to her? See her even?"

"I can. You can't, I take it." Vinnie said she couldn't see the dead. "I can. Did you know that before coming here?"

Vinnie stood up. She was slightly dizzy and terrified, but she stood straight now. "I'm sorry to have bothered you, Mr. Riley. I'm sure that without your help, the Bruces will win a suit or two, and that might satisfy them for a while."

"I asked you a question, Miss Graham. Did you know that we were a house of necromancers when you came here?"

She hadn't, and she doubted that she would have come had she known. But as she made her way to the door, nearly running now, she could only think to get away, get her little family away. But Mitch stepped in front of her just as she reached for the door.

Backing away from him, she didn't even look at him as she answered. "I didn't, as a matter of fact. I wish I had known, but I'm guessing that there really isn't any way that you could advertise such a thing and expect people to believe you. I'd very much like to go."

"She's not here right now. Steele sent her away. For now." The relief was profound. And before she realized what was happening, she felt herself being lifted up. Hugo had her. But when she looked into his face, it wasn't that of her bodyguard, but of Mitch Riley.

"Let me down." He held her still, taking her to what she thought was the kitchen. "There is nothing in here that I can use to make me feel better. I'd very much like to be left to go please."

"Hush." Vinnie started to snap at him, but she was sat down on a table and a wet cloth was slapped in her hand. "What does she have over you? It must be big for a badassed vamp like you to get yourself all worked up about."

Vinnie laid the dishtowel on the table and stood up. She was stronger now, more than likely due to being so angry. But when she started to leave the room, Mitch grabbed her by the arm. Vinnie felt her temper snap, and she let her power go.

Nick.

Also Available in the Justice Series:

Available Now

Before You Go...

Share your voice and help guide other readers to these wonderful books. Even if it's only a line or two your reviews help readers discover the author's books so they can continue creating stories that you'll love. Login and leave a review.

AWARD WINNING, BESTSELLING AUTHOR

Kathi Barton, author of the bestselling series Force of Nature, lives in Nashport, Ohio with her husband Paul. In addition to writing full time Kathi likes to spend time with her eight grandkids, three children and three children-in-laws. She writes to relax and have fun.

Her muse, a cross between Jimmy Stewart and Hugh Jackman brings them to life for her readers in a way that has them coming back time and again for more. Her favorite genre is paranormal romance with a great deal of spice. You can visit Kathi on line and drop her an email if you'd like. She loves hearing from her fans. aaronskiss@gmail.com.

Follow Kathi on her blog:
http://kathisbartonauthor.blogspot.com/